THE CONDUIT

BY

CHRYSELLE BROWN

For Tim, Kristian and Luke
With gratitude and love always.

THE CONDUIT

Chapter 1

Hektor Xanthis was in the middle of a crisis. The men sitting around the table were listening intently as Xanthis talked. They were members of his board of directors and were giving him their full attention. There was fear and unease in the room. They had been informed early yesterday morning that there was an emergency with Odysseus Shipping and had been summoned post-haste for a meeting here in Cyprus. Now the ten men, heads of Hektor's vast shipping empire, were grave and silent in the face of this unprecedented event- the threat by persons unknown of creating a series of deliberate oil spills of global proportions in the ocean using Odysseus oil tankers!

Hektor was talking, questioning the level of security being undertaken by the different heads of his corporation. Hektor said, 'The reason you are all here in person is so this information can be contained within the room. We must maintain the utmost security. Now, the threat received by the London office was contained in an electronic mail message - it is with MI5 and the good news is they have assured me it will be a matter of hours before they trace the culprits.

The terrorists' message guaranteed an oil spill within the next month. Their demand is that I personally remove myself from the political arena here in Cyprus. I can say without any hesitation that I will never give in to any threat, terrorist or otherwise. However, I mean to make damned sure that my personal safety, and that of all of you is maintained at the highest level. I have instructed the police accordingly.

'Tell me, Stelios, what is being done about matters at your end? Have you got a breakdown regarding worst possible-case scenario?' asked Hektor

'Kyrios Hektor' said Stelios the general manager of his London office, 'On behalf of all present, I believe we are in agreement to increase our security measures to the highest level. We have already set things in motion. We have warned the port authorities and the police and Intelligence services in more than 20 countries. We cannot control, however, what happens in mid-ocean. Our fear is the open sea where the terrorists can seize the vessel and force us into shallow waters. Grounding of the carrier is inevitable, causing in most cases, major damage to the hull and the cargo of oil therein. Even if no damage is sustained, just restarting the engines and attempting to get into deeper waters may cause a hole in a tanker. In either event, oil will start to leak into the ocean, causing as you know losses of billions of pounds in a clean-up operation and moreover, immense damage to marine life and the environment. The whole world will be in an uproar!

As you are all aware two of our ULCC – ultra large crude carriers – containing 2 million barrels of oil are the most vulnerable to attack as they are the single-hulled variety. Only one layer between the bottom and the oil. Just one crack to cause a leak. The rest of our ships are double-hulled with two layers. The oil in the double-hulled is stored in the middle layer which protects it from accidental damage. It would take a sizeable team of men and specialised equipment to breach its outer layer to get to the middle. They could not escape detection.'

Hektor said, 'Can we put the two single-hulled in dry dock until the threat is nullified?'

'I thought of that and checked on the vessels workloads. We are at full stretch, Kyrios Xanthis. It will be another three months before they are free of their commitments'

Hektor turned to the men in the room, 'As of last month, I have ordered another two double-hulled vessels to replace the single ones- the law demands that by 2010 all vessels are double–hulled, but the bad news is that they won't be available for another two years. No, we will just have to ride the threat out and hope that this is an empty hoax. Although, I confess to having a bad feeling about all of this. I believe this sort of threat, in one way or another, will continue given the current climate in Cyprus. I have initiated protective measures for now. Let's hope they are sufficient. Ok everyone your instructions are in the files in front of you. We will meet again tonight. I believe most of you will be leaving tomorrow.'

Hektor turned to his assistant, 'Next I wish to be briefed in full as to the consequences of a major oil spill. The last one, I believe was enough to fill a hundred and twenty-five Olympic-sized swimming pools!'

Hektor's assistant said, 'Kyrios Hektor, a Mr. Parker from London is on your personal line and wishes to speak with you urgently'

Hektor strode down the corridor to his office and picked up the phone- he knew it was the MI5 man Parker, he said, 'any progress?'

Parker said, 'We traced the email to a lone individual- a disgruntled ex-employee of yours- name of Toby Stewart. No known affiliations in London. We believe the man is being used by persons unknown, who are operating outside of the UK. Unfortunately we were too late to question the man as he has escaped the country. We believe he is heading in your direction or rather north of your borders, to Northern Cyprus.

Our concern is that he might have associations in that part of the world, part of a larger group of radicals who are upset at your involvement in politics, hence the demand that you remove yourself from the political arena- regret to say that we cannot rely on Interpol to apprehend the man as you know we have no jurisdiction in Northern Cyprus, it being an unrecognised country- so criminals there are pretty much free to roam with impunity. We do maintain some sources, however, and will be keeping you informed'

Minutes later, Hektor put the phone down and walked quickly back to the boardroom where the ten men were still reading through the files. Hektor told them of the latest developments. Hektor did not tell them of his own conviction that it was not a personal vendetta by Toby Stewart but part of a much larger picture, encompassing Northern Cyprus and its Turkish masters. Hektor had the feeling the hunt was on and he was the prime quarry!

Chapter 2

Fran Mitchell read aloud the next name on her list. The room was full and there was a low hum of conversation. Fran looked around the room at the people waiting. The clinic was full today. 'Wow', she thought, 'who is that?!' Fran stared at the woman for more than an instant before collecting herself, she called the name out again, waited to escort the man who answered, then hurried to tell Jane, her co-worker to go and take a look at the woman. Fran had never seen anyone more beautiful.

'I wonder what she's in for?' she asked Jane. Fran thought that amongst the odd mismatch of people that was customary, the woman shone like a precious jewel. Jane was curious and went to the desk to get a good vantage point. From behind the pot plant on the desk she peered at the woman. Long black hair and beautiful translucent skin, huge green eyes and full red lips, Jane while assimilating these features suddenly became aware that she was staring. She hastily turned her eyes away

'What do you think it is?' she asked the approaching Fran, 'What's wrong with her? I must say we do get all sorts in here. Oh, I do like her outfit, that blue velvet jacket toned with the blue and emerald skirt. She looks really exotic. Do you remember her name?'

Fran answered as she looked down the list. 'I think she said, Cathy-- umm here it is Cathy Burkert'.

Cathy, the object of their attention, did not notice anything unusual. She was used to being stared at. Besides she was too busy listening to her friend, the psychic healer, Matt Mallard. He was talking with that dark velvet voice. God, he was sexy, she thought. Tall and dark and exuding masculinity. She remembered their one sexual encounter. A golden day, sepia tinted sketches in her head of naked bodily outlines- did they actually do the deed? - make glorious passionate love?- she could not remember.

So much had happened since. All she knew was that they shared this special bond. He told her so repeatedly. He had talked to her about it,

'It's a psycho-kinetic connection - Psychokinesis literally meaning mind-movement, basically controlling objects with the mind. There are books written about the subject. Have you read the ones I suggested?'

Cathy had read about it, trying to understand this scary paranormal world. Then one Sunday a few weeks ago, she had attempted to move objects by concentrating on them, which she had reasoned was what psychokinesis was about-remote mental influence. Firstly she had got hold of a couple of spoons and tried to imitate Uri Geller the famous extra-sensory perceptionist.

After concentrating on them in turn for about ten minutes Cathy had been terrified to see the spoons bending. She then took an unused key and the same thing happened. She tried again with a clothes hanger with the same result. Cathy gathered all the metal bits she could find. An hour later, she gazed astounded at them. The metal was undoubtedly bent. Cathy gathered them up, rushed outside and deposited them in the bin. She sat down, feeling quite shaken. She calmed herself and thought: So I can bend metal. For a while Cathy stared into space, quite shocked at her ability, then resolved to accept this facet of her make-up and decided not to be overwhelmed by it. There was no-one to talk to about it, apart from the healer and he was always far too pushy- forcing her to acknowledge her psychic gifts. Surely that sort of thing was a bit whacky! Something abnormal, not at all fitting for an every-day, normal person. She resolved to put the spoon-bending out of her mind.

She was pleased she had got rid of the items and had told the healer half-laughingly about the episode.

But Matt Mallard was not amused. He said, 'We share an ability way beyond just bending spoons. Time will teach you to understand and explore the gifts you have. For now it's enough that you are aware that you are not only psychokinetic but you are a telepathist as well.'

At her blank look he added, 'Telepathy is the ability to communicate without the use of the five known senses. You and I are one of the few people in the world who can do this. I can read minds, other people's thoughts pop into my head. You can too. You told me so recently'. He looked at her. She didn't look surprised.

Cathy looked down. She had not been surprised. Just taken aback at having a name put to something she had lived with all her life. She had known that thoughts would pop into her head, other people's thoughts. Especially when they were thinking about her or talking about her – a phone call or unfolding events, a conversation, then or later would confirm her intuition.

But she had never questioned it. When she had first met Matt Mallard and he had always seemed to know what she was thinking, Cathy had accepted it as nothing out of the ordinary, albeit feeling a great deal of frustration at his pre-empting her on every occasion with what she was going to say. Now here he was putting a name to it. Saying that she was a telepathist! If this is true, she thought, then I should be able to read *his* mind. But I never can.

The healer had watched her and said, 'One day I'll tell you why' He had smiled and tapped his nose. 'I've taken bloody good care you don't' he added to himself.
He held her hand 'I intend to look after you, lovely one. Be very careful with the knowledge I have given you about yourself. I have confided in you a great secret- our shared abilities. These could be used for nefarious purposes, people could use and abuse our thought processes. But I've said enough. All you need to know is that I will be here for you. I promise'.

Cathy had started to be concerned that she was different from other people but at his words she had melted. This was so special to her, so very special - all the more because it was secret. She hadn't told anybody about their relationship. To confide in anyone would spoil the magic. And it was magical. When he was with her she sparkled, filled with humour and fun. She had been happy and had considered herself so unbelievably lucky to have found Matt. But that was five months ago.

Lately it had changed. When had it started to change? He had started being sharp with her. His tone sometimes had a cruel edge. She focused on what he was saying. His voice was soft, he was almost whispering.

'I know that your father was a liar and a cheat' Shock washed over her. Her eyes dilated. Her breathing turned shallow. She had the impression of shards of glass hard and sharp. It had been five years. Five years of forgetting and now this. Her heart sank with despair. The familiar pain started deep in the pit of her stomach. Shame washed over her. She couldn't bear to go back and remember those awful times of her childhood and teenage years. She thought no-one would ever find out. She had thought she was safe. Desperately, she tried to divert her thoughts. But it was no use. He was in her mind. She had to answer.

She said, 'No. No. He wasn't. It wasn't like that'

But he was relentless. 'Yes, he was. He cheated people out of hundreds of thousands of pounds. He ruined lives, Cathy, people lost their life-savings.'

The memories flooded back, the shouting and the screaming, the child's feelings of helplessness. Her entire body squirmed.

'It was legitimate. He had a business. They were investors', she said desperately.

He spoke harshly, 'Investors who believed and trusted your father. They put their life-savings into a venture they believed to be genuine. But he never got the business off the ground, did he Cathy? Why did he never open his factory? The factory that was to produce essential essences for perfumes- he was getting into a huge multi-million industry, the perfume business. Your father sold the investors the idea, took their money and never did anything. He was a criminal.' His lips twisted, he spoke savagely

'That makes you Cathy, my beauty, nothing but common Italian-Irish trash. But you had me fooled. You seemed to have it all.' He laughed and held his fingers up in the air, counting them off, 'You with your looks, your vivacity, your intelligence, your elegance, your lineage - is that true, he laughed sarcastically the Italian countess bit – ha! I intend to find out, all of it. There is no escape.' The shards of glass were blue now, ice-like. 'What do you have to say, Cathy?'

Cathy, however had gone mentally, spiralling down into this great hole. She was frightened and shaking. The healer was a psychic and a telepathist. She must not think in case he divined her thoughts. She must not remember. Think of something else. Birdsong, that's it, can you hear the birdsong? Oh no the President-elect intruded. Somehow she always associated him with the harmony of birdsong. My God shut him out quick. She couldn't let the healer find out about the President. She had promised that she would never tell. Panicking, she tried to think of something, anything else but her mind would not let go of the images called up by the psychic's words. And her father's face swam in front of her. Cathy's mind began to drift.

Cathy Burkert was now eight years old. She knelt in front of her father helping him with his shoes. She was terrified of him. He was a big man and could quite easily strike her. He often did if she annoyed him.

She eased the shoe on gently, taking great care to let her small fingers create gaps so that his big foot could slip into the shoe easily. She breathed a sigh of relief when she had the foot in. The second foot was nearly in but she pinched his foot at the last instant. She flinched in anticipation of the thwack with big green eyes staring up at him in fear and dread but this time he didn't notice, his mind was obviously on other things. He looked funny, thought Cathy almost furtive, and he was being kind telling her where he was going, 'I'm off to the city', he said, 'I know your mum has taken the other three with her to her sisters. Leah will look after you.' While he was talking he was concealing something in his hand. He rolled the object in the palm of his hand and she wondered what it was.

At that moment, Leah was calling out to her from the kitchen telling her that tea was ready. As she sat down to wolf down the bread and butter pudding and drink her tea, Cathy automatically made the sign of the cross as she had been taught to do in the strict Catholic household, but in her mind she intoned the words, 'God be praised, my belly is about to be raised 6 inches off the ground.' It was Cathy's way of rebelling, just thinking sinful thoughts.

She heard Leah, at the sink, muttering under her breath. 'Why can't that great fat man put on his shoes himself? There's nothing wrong with him. He's just too fat to bend. So he has the children doing it for him. The good Lord have mercy on them. He's a tyrant, there's no mistaking – the way he beats them. And not just with his hands- with his belt and the cane too!! And the madam too. I've seen him raise his hands to her. I'm scared of the day he turns on me. I won't wait for that. Oh no siree, not with my wages absent for the last three months. If there's no money, I have to move on.' Cathy could barely hear what Leah was saying. Cathy was especially good around Leah, hoping that Leah would like her, but Leah ignored her most of the time. She preferred Cathy's older sister Fiona.

Fiona had once told Cathy out of Leah's earshot that Leah was middle-aged! Cathy thought that Leah had a permanent sour look on her face and didn't make a good job of looking after everything in the house. Leah lived in one of the attic rooms in the sprawling house and being nanny to the children and overseeing the house were part of her duties. She supervised the two local women who came in from the village and who helped her with the cooking and the cleaning, although

Mum said that she couldn't trust them to do it properly, and went about the house cleaning after them.

Cathy caught the last words Leah uttered. 'Oh don't leave Leah. We have money. Look how Mummy gave you some lovely new dresses for Christmas.' Leah answered 'Humph!' and busied herself at the sink. She muttered under her breath 'Your Dad is a harsh man, young missy and him so respected by the Church. Why, the Parish Priest, Father Callaghan thinks the world of him, so do the neighbours and his friends. He is a good man for the world to see and gives kindly to people but he is terrible to you children. Children should be disciplined but to see the weal's on your arms from the cane and the belt leaving bloody trails across your backs is terrible. It's not right but it isn't my place to interfere. Oh no, I keep my mouth shut.' She turned to Cathy. 'And if you've been listening with them flappers, don't you go telling your mother and father what I've just said. For I'll get the sack and how is your mother going to manage, all on her own'.

Cathy silently understood. She remembered something she had heard the grown-ups talking about "Daddy was an orphan. The monks in the orphanage used to punish the children by beating them. That's why

Daddy beats us when we are naughty. It's all our fault, Leah.'

Leah frowned ferociously and said briskly, "Eat that pudding and drink your tea. Your Mum and your brothers and sister will be back soon and will be wanting theirs.'

Leah was a simple unemotional woman and had worked for the family ever since they had arrived from Italy three years ago. Her job working for the family was just that – a job to quit at anytime she found it not to her liking, she felt faint pity for the madam and the children but she was always on tenterhooks when the master was around. He was arrogant and demanding and all the staff were terrified of him. There was a gardener, Cormack and Joseph the general factotum who helped with the upkeep of the buildings. Theo, the chauffeur, was the one Leah liked best. Leah was looking forward to their natter later when all four of them took their dinner in the kitchen after serving the family theirs in the dining-room.

Cathy was enjoying today now that Daddy had gone out. Daddy was always home for tea on a Saturday and Sunday. In fact, it was unusual to be the only one home for tea. But she had the mumps and was *not allowed to infect her young cousins. So she couldn't go with the rest to visit her Aunt. Cathy loved tea-time. Normally, during the week after Theo had fetched the children from school they would all be seated around the table noisy, shuffling and demanding. Mum would have cajoled Leah into baking something special for them and the children enjoyed the magical half-hour of tea-time before commencing their home-work. Mum was really strict when it came to home-work and would not let them play until the work was finished. 'Mama Lucia Marco di Laurentis' Cathy said aloud. Cathy always pictured her mother in warm toffee taffeta and creamy old lace- a favourite dress her mother wore for grand parties. Cathy got her pen and writing book and lovingly wrote her mother's name out.*

Chapter 3

Lucia Marco di Laurentis looked in the little lipstick mirror and applied some lip gloss. She sighed and thought that lately she was being too introspective. Thoughts of Italy and the comforting presence of her mother and father in these difficult times beckoned. Her parents had been so supportive and had sent Giorgio to help. Poor Mama and Papa! For this to happen to them, to all of us! We had led such a privileged life, now only the title remains- for me anyway.

Lucia had a noble lineage going back two hundred years, her father currently held the title of Count Rudolfo Marco di Laurentis. Her family were modestly wealthy, their income mainly derived from the land and the small perfumery they owned. In previous years the family had been extremely rich but their fortunes had dwindled during the last war and had never recovered. Lucia was a fine woman, quiet and refined. Her parents had had her educated entirely in a Convent in England but when she was seventeen and had been due to return home to Italy, her schooling being finished, she happened to go as usual with the nuns to the local parish church for Sunday Mass. That's when Simon first saw her. He fell in love with her at first sight, a love that was to be his only redeeming feature in later years. He made sure he was introduced to the dark-haired young girl by the priest and she, shy and adorable responded to his Irish blarney and was persuaded to visit the Church for the next Sunday. Simon was working for the local solicitors office where he was a secretary handling all the correspondence.

He was now 25 years old and had held the job for the last 5 years. He had left the orphanage with secretarial qualifications and after working at a couple of low-paid jobs, had applied to the solicitors firm and had steadily worked his way up and now the promotion of office manager was in the offing. Simon was ambitious and he was hard-working. He intended to go far but for now he was in love and intended to marry Lucia. Lucia was due to return to Italy in a month so he had to move quickly. He saw her every Sunday, visited her at the Convent where the nuns though extremely protective of the girl didn't see the harm at them taking tea and walking in the garden.

Lucia duly went back to Italy but Simon fearful that her parents might have potential bridegrooms in mind, soon followed her and made himself known to her parents through the local church. As a potential suitor he had little to offer apart from his good looks, his bearing and his air of going places. First he had to get Count Rudolfo, Lucia's father to trust him. He sensed a business opportunity was there for the taking. Simon knew that to establish trust, would be no easy task so he decided after a week he would have to go back to England withdraw all his savings and move permanently to Italy to woo Lucia's father. Simon was unconcerned. After many a confrontation with authority in the orphanage, and having escaped each encounter with hardly a scratch from the cane-wielding monks, mainly due to the fact that Simon inspired confidence and people he met were wont to trust him implicitly, he knew it was only a matter of time before the Count succumbed to his flattery.

Simon thought a week should do it. In fact, it took Count Rudolfo a good two weeks to offer him a job within the small perfumery, persuaded by his wife Antoinetta that he was doing the right thing. Simon had charmed Antoinetta with a few choice phrases of Italian *he had learnt. Simon flourished. He worked hard, learnt the perfumery business inside out and at the end of two years Rudolfo was persuaded to let Simon and Lucia marry.*

Ten years went by. The Count relied on Simon absolutely and was quite content to take a back seat and have Simon run the business. The only bone of contention between them was that Simon wanted to expand the company by setting up a factory in England to produce the essential essences needed for the perfumes. It would be far cheaper than to import the expensive ingredients from Holland, their nearest supplier and Simon who hankered for England and complete control of his own outfit saw himself as the perfect person to take over the management of that end of the market

Rudolfo saw the business sense of such a move but he and Antoinetta did not want to lose their daughter, Lucia and by now four grandchildren. However Simon was persistent and finally wore Rudolfo down. Reluctantly, Rudolfo resigned himself to them moving to England. Lucia had only one sister Francesca who was married to Giorgio, an architect and they had three children. So the old man felt not entirely bereft.

Simon and Lucia set sail for England. Lucia was happy to be back in England, the place of her schooling and her youth and she soon settled in making friends among the local community and the various church groups.

The sound of a name being called brought Cathy back to the present. It wasn't hers. Cathy looked at the healer. She was aware that for the first time in her life she was communicating intimate details of her family to the healer, an outsider. She pulled herself up as she became aware of the deep tension in her stomach. 'What would Mum say about telling a relative stranger all of her childhood history- stuff that her mother had insisted was to remain within the family- but he was so good', she thought. So good at extracting information. I have never told anyone these things before. Yet I think and he knows.

The healer said, 'Relax, Cathy, don't be afraid of this communication. Tell me, what do you remember?'

It was alright to think of this bit, she thought. Cathy said 'I remember the excitement of the sea-voyage to England and all those trunks, full of mystery and promise, being opened after our arrival.' She smiled.

A smile that radiated innocence, thought the dark-skinned young man watching her. He had sat down quietly in the chair opposite, almost immediately after Cathy had taken her seat. He pressed the button on the sophisticated recorder in his jacket pocket and hoped the conversation was coming through loud and clear to his mate in the car park.

The clothes were musty and smelled of salt-spray from the voyage but they contained all her familiar belongings and she was happy. The house was big and rambling and the garden had a secret enclosure, which was colourful in the summer with trailing wisteria and proved a perfect hideout from her older brother and sister, Mark and Fiona. She and her younger brother, Harry would play for many a long hour in what she thought of as her secret garden, her wisteria sanctuary.

Smooth, so soft, the healer's voice said, 'Are you eight years old again, Cathy? Tell me first about school and then what happened that day when you had the mumps? You said that Leah baked you a bread and butter pudding. What happened next? Why do you remember that day?'

The healer watched her eyes, those beautiful green orbs looked blank. His look was one of satisfaction. 'Good,' he muttered 'now....you said you were ill and off school?' The mention of school jogged Cathy's memory, her train of thought as if uninterrupted.

Better finish that homework straight after tea, thought Cathy before Mum gets back. Even though she was considered ill, Mum had said she could manage a bit of reading. Cathy loved reading anyway and she was looking forward to her book. It made up for not being able to go and see her cousins. She went upstairs to her room to get her book but as she passed her mother's room she noticed through the open door her mother's jewellery box was out on the dressing table. Strange, thought Cathy for Mum to forget to put it back in the safe. Ooh it would be nice to have a look inside. Lucia would let the girls try on her rings and necklaces so Cathy felt no qualms in opening the heavy lid of the silver casket.

She spent a good ten minutes poking about in the case but some of the stuff wasn't there. What has happened to the sapphire ring and the heavy necklace. They were Cathy's favourites. I must ask Mum.

Perhaps Mum's worn it today or it might have got lost. Suddenly, a shaft of extreme anxiety gripped Cathy. She quickly closed the lid and ran out of the room. She thought she had heard the front door opening. Had the others returned? If Cathy had turned her head to look back into the room she would have seen the antique silver case had begun to twist out of shape but Cathy never knew.

Now sitting with Matt with a knowledge of her own ability to influence objects, Cathy remembered her mother being baffled and questioning of her daughters as to how the case came to be misshapen.

The mystery had remained unsolved until now. Thanks to the healer making her aware of her abilities. Cathy thought, is my metal-bending associated with my intuition and the stress I feel? I hope that somebody can answer my questions today. Or, Heaven knows what might happen to stuff around me!

Cathy remembered going downstairs from her mother's bedroom. She was waiting by the front door for her siblings to return. Cathy was grateful that Mum's sister, Aunt Francesca had been around in the last six weeks with Uncle Giorgio and the three cousins. They had come to help Daddy with the business, which

Cathy overheard from a conversation between her mum and Uncle Giorgio was failing, but they didn't seem to be helping Daddy much. The children had to tread on eggshells when he came home from the factory, just in case he got angry and hit them or pinched them in his frustration with his day. The pinches were really, really painful. Cathy stroked her tummy in remembrance. He would grab hold of the flesh around the navel and twist the flesh so hard that the children would scream in agony, and he would all the while berate them with harsh words.

'You good for nothing' he would shout, his mouth twisting viciously, 'are you deaf, dumb and stupid? Why are you running in the house when you are expressly forbidden to do so?' or on another occasion 'What were you doing with your cousin Paolo?' He lifted up Cathy's skirt and tugged it back down

'Nothing, Daddy, nothing. We were just playing with his aeroplane'

'Aeroplane, my foot, you watch it you dirty little girl- get down on your knees and stay there'.

Cathy wondered what she had done. She felt the sexual undertone of condemnation to his words but at eight couldn't comprehend it. She did feel dirty as though she had done something wrong. She also hoped he wouldn't forget that she was kneeling down. The last time he had, and she had been there for three hours, and only when Mum had come across her unexpectedly, was Cathy told to get up.

'My poor Cathy, the healer whispered, 'why was your father so cruel to you?'

'It was because of the business.'

Cathy's green eyes were unfocused. However, despite Matt staring at her fixedly, a stray unconnected thought relating to the present moment entered her head – She thought, I haven't thought about the past so logically before. It's because of the healer, he is with me. He is my safety cushion – a buffer against the pain of remembering. Cathy felt grateful. She told him more.

Simon wasn't doing well. Being in sole charge of the company, with no-one to oversee him, he lacked the motivation and endeavour to succeed on his own. In Italy his weight had steadily increased and now his obesity added to his slothfulness. Times were bad generally. In the beginning Simon had set up and expanded the business into providing essences not just for perfumes but for food manufacturing and he had been very successful adding name after illustrious name to his client list.

But in the last year business had started to drop drastically when Simon's Dutch competitors dropped their prices to match Simon's —besides the Dutch were a long-established company with prompt delivery schedules, Simon's deliveries were erratic, he lacked a good foreman, and more importantly lacked the business acumen to deal with the crisis. Simon who looked for financial assistance from Rudolfo in Italy was told there would be no more infusion of cash. In fact, just today Rudolfo had given him an ultimatum. Simon had a month to wind things up as it was no longer feasible for Rudolfo to prolong the operation in England. Rudolfo was resigned and did not blame Simon. It made good business sense to cut one's losses and Simon could always come back to Italy. Rudolfo for one would be very happy to see all of them safely under his roof once again. Rudolfo decided he could bear the financial loss. He missed Lucia and the children and that meant Francesca and Giorgio would be home as well. As a matter of fact, that's the main reason that Giorgio was there to help Simon wind things up. But for Simon it was a blow to his monumental pride. He felt cheated. He had worked so hard. How dare Rudolfo shut down the business? He wasn't going to go to his father-in-law with his tail between his legs. No fear. He had had a taste for being his own boss and he had decided he liked the power and status it gave him. Why, he was invited to all the houses of the top echelon in the neighbourhood. He worked indefatigably for church events and his reputation as a good man spread. Simon was well-liked, he was affable and was full of stories and charm. Lucia's title impressed the snobs and both Simon and Lucia led a hectic social life. Simon liked his life and he wasn't about to let it change.

No, Simon knew exactly what he was going to do. He was going to start up on his own in competition with his father-in-law. He had the perfect scheme. He had no savings as he had lived the high life whilst in his father-in-law's employ. Besides, he had always thought of Rudolfo as the cash-cow, should he need it. But now Rudolfo wouldn't budge. As a result, Simon needed investment and he needed it quick. Simon put his plans into action. He had compiled a list of would-be investors from the scores of contacts he had acquired and having sounded them out he was confident they would agree to his plan. Quite simply Simon was going to the competition. He was going to join forces with the Dutch and produce the essential essences with their collaboration. Everything seemed to be going smoothly.

Cathy paused and said to the healer, 'I have often wondered if my father had achieved his business plan, would he have been a kinder person?'

For as a child and in her teens Cathy was in a state of constant tension. Naturally as a child she would forget whilst playing and reading and when she was in school but as soon as she saw her father she would walk quietly so he wouldn't hear her. She hid so he couldn't see her. She was convinced she was a bad person and that's the reason he beat her and the other children. *She suddenly remembered her father concealing something in his hand when she was eight years old. He had gone into town and returned only just in time for dinner and had been laughing and joking. Mum had been her usual self. Leah, however had hugged Cathy. That was unusual. Cathy remembered hugs. She usually got no signs of affection from either her father and whilst her mother was caring, she was not demonstrative, so when she was hugged by sour Leah, something was different. Perhaps Leah had been paid, remembering Leah's words earlier. Cathy was eight years old but suddenly she knew the reason why she had felt so anxious when looking at Mummy's jewellery box. She knew what Daddy had done. Daddy had taken Mum's jewellery- the ring and necklace missing from the box. He had sold it for money. Did Mummy know? Or had he stolen it?*

The dark skinned man opposite stood up and made his way to the gents toilet. He wanted to listen to the playback.

Chapter 4

Cathy was aware the healer was watching her intently as she divulged her past. Oh it was so hopeless she thought. She could not stop the torrent of memories. I wish he'd leave me alone but could I do without him? He made her feel so good. She relied on him. He talked to her about politics, religion, about her job. He made her feel as though her opinion counted. 'Come on Cathy. What happened to your father? Tell me all. You know I am the only person in the world you can trust.'

Cathy looked around her but her eyes were unseeing. The room was full of people but Cathy could not focus. She seemed to be in a trance.

The healer looked at her, his eyes boring into hers, 'Tell me Cathy, all of it. What happened?'

Cathy didn't answer and instead thought of the reason she was here today. Her metal bending and the associated trauma was getting out of hand – it seemed as though once being aware of it she was unconsciously concentrating on metal items around her- the spoons in the flat were fast disappearing and her flatmate had started to complain. Cathy hadn't owned up for fear of being labelled a freak but the matter was becoming of great concern to her. She had decided to seek help.

And here she was sitting in a white-walled room, posters displaying all the latest aids to recovery on the big notice-board in front of her, with the healer saying, 'Don't worry my sweet, with me here, the metal bending is in control- it happens only when you are on your own and experiencing a little intense reaction- probably boyfriend trouble. Is he anybody I know?'

Cathy went red and looked hastily away.

Mallard smiled, 'Never mind now, tell me the rest. It will help to make this anxiety go away.'

Cathy succumbed. She dredged her memory bank.

Just then her mobile phone rang. The noise was so loud in that place. Cathy answered, almost whispering. Cathy out of the corner of her eye became aware of the healer leaving. She was alone. His muttered last words of 'There's somebody else trying to get in on this communication between us. I'm leaving' impinged on Cathy's mind as she listened to the voice speaking Italian at the end of the phone.

The caller wanted to arrange a meeting. Cathy agreed on a date and time. The call concerned Cathy's job as a freelance interpreter. She spoke fluent Italian which she had learnt from Lucia. When she was twenty-one Cathy went to University and studied Classical Studies with emphasis on Ancient Greek. She studied Modern Greek in her spare time and progressed to being virtually fluent. After leaving University she had decided she would like to work as a freelance interpreter. It had been hard trying to establish herself but her savings had stood her in good stead for the first couple of months.

Thereafter by sheer determination and networking at the Italian, Greek and Cyprus embassies, she had managed to get an assignment. Business picked up fairly rapidly especially due to Cathy being prepared to work all hours. Now she was often called upon by businessmen to translate important documents, to interpret in meetings, some of them highly confidential. The Embassies had her details on file and would call upon her services. Sometimes she was invited to official Embassy functions to act as an interpreter for visiting dignitaries. That was how she met Hektor Xanthis.

Cathy had dressed carefully that evening. She wore her honey-beige silk. The dress swirled around her, sensuously. She knew she looked good. She had arranged to meet the Bishop, her client, at the Cyprus embassy official trade function, to which the Bishop had been invited. The room was full of elegantly dressed people. One of the embassy aides who had been informed of Cathy's presence, ushered her towards the tall, bearded man, the Bishop, in his imposing robes and headdress. Next Cathy was introduced to the Bishop's assistant who informed her of the job she was required to do. A couple of pages of ancient text needed urgent translation. These pages had only come to light whilst the Bishop had been in London and he needed them quickly. Cathy whose speciality had been Ancient Greek at University, suddenly felt nervous.

She listened while the assistant told her how important this find of papers had been to the Bishop and he had hoped it would give some clue to his ancestral name, which would settle a land dispute between two families.

'We are waiting for a gentleman who is the other interested party', he added. He suggested they withdraw to an ante-chamber. Ten minutes later Cathy was ensconced in a red leather chair and was poring over the manuscript. It had a protective plastic cover but Cathy could see that it was very old and very fragile. Cathy made out the words with difficulty. Oh dear, she thought, the Bishop is going to be disappointed. She looked up and stared straight into very black eyes.

'Hektor Xanthis', he said suavely as he shook her hand. She had been so intent on the translation that she hadn't noticed him enter the room. Cathy saw there were other men in the room too. Cathy's gaze returned to those black eyes. She felt a strange touch of

breathlessness. A sense of eternity. She looked down and saw the papers in her lap.

Cathy collected herself, stood up and the Bishop, the assistant and Xanthis looked at her expectantly. She explained the contents of the document to the men standing before her. The translation did include a name but it was not the Bishop's. The name was that of the scribe who had indicated that he was copying the information from a pre-existing record. Cathy had wondered at the reason for copying such a mundane matter - merely a record of the family's ancient worship to the goddess Aphrodite and a list of votive offerings. Perhaps it had been at a time when Pagans had to hide their beliefs for fear of reprisals from Christian fanatics, thought Cathy fancifully. She did not suggest her thoughts to her audience. She said, 'There is not a whisper of an ancestral name in these pages. I'm sorry'

Cathy said to the Bishop's Assistant, 'I will email you the full transcript first thing tomorrow.'

Xanthis said to the Bishop, 'This has been a waste of time. As you know I have the paperwork to prove that the tract of land had been sold to my family a century ago. My staff have made copies of the relevant papers. They will give them to you.'

The Bishop's face was crestfallen. Hektor on the other hand gave no hint of the satisfaction he felt that the land would stay in his possession. He spoke charmingly and persuasively to the Bishop but the old man turned away.

Hektor turned to Cathy, 'I had hoped the Bishop would have put aside our differences. But it is not to be.' He shrugged. 'Let's put this matter behind us. Will you join us for dinner?' Cathy felt a rush of excitement. She felt a frisson, a strange enchantment. Cathy thought, Careful. Steady girl.

Nevertheless, she agreed and then the other men in the room were being introduced and Cathy was being escorted to the waiting Mercedes by a young man who introduced himself as Stelios. Cathy barely had time to register the plush customised interior of the car before they were drawing up before the restaurant. Hektor was waiting outside. He had obviously arrived in another vehicle, slightly ahead of them. He followed Cathy inside and indicated a table where several women were seated. Introductions were made and Cathy understood these were the wives of the men whom she had been introduced to and who accompanied them now.

Hektor seated her on his right with Stelios on the other side of her. Cathy looked at Hektor's right hand, he wore a wedding ring on it, as was the custom in Greece. Cathy couldn't stop herself. She said to Hektor, 'your wife, is she not here?' Hektor laughed and said, 'Tonight I am a bachelor. I'm only here in London for a couple of days, on business. My wife is in Cyprus. These men are from the London offices.'

Throughout the dinner Hektor was very attentive to her when he was able, as the demands on his time from the others present was in the nature of a football game, fast and furious. Stelios on her other side explained, 'When you are as necessary to the shipping empire of Odysseus as Hektor is, your attention span to each person is miniscule' Cathy looked blank. 'Oh I gather the Bishop did not explain who Hektor Xanthis is. He is the owner of Odysseus Shipping- you know the shipping line that owns oil tankers, cargo boats, pleasure cruisers and yachts all around the world.'

Cathy was not impressed. She had had enough experience as a child of the world of finance and she knew what heartache befell the people who did not succeed. Stelios saw the tight expression on her face *and wondered a little at this woman. She had looked repelled. Most women liked Hektor Xanthis, they found him charming and attentive. They liked the power and the money and Stelios had heard he was more than generous to his women. But this young woman was different.*

He whispered to his wife seated on his right and she leaned across him and said to Cathy, 'My dear, Stelios tells me you are an interpreter. And that you know ancient Greek and modern Greek. Quite an achievement. Not a lot of people even know they are quite separate languages. Only a few similar words. Have you been to Cyprus?'

Cathy said, 'No but I have been to Greece as part of my degree.'

For the next few minutes they discussed Cathy's visit and then Stelios' wife, Maria said, 'You must visit Cyprus. We will welcome you there. With your education, you would be very interested in our Ancient sites.'

Cathy paused before continuing the conversation and Hektor on her left touched her arm and said softly, 'Give your card to Stelios. I would like to see you again'

Cathy felt a sense of joy but she quickly squashed it. She couldn't believe the way she felt. He's married, she thought. He's also at least a decade older and he has girls like me for breakfast. She suddenly made a decision, she wasn't going to have anything to do with him. She decided to leave as soon as she was able and as soon as dinner was over, she declined a coffee and made her excuses 'I'm sorry I have to leave, I have an appointment first thing in the morning'.

Hektor stood up, took her hand and wished her goodbye along with the others. Stelios accompanied her outside to hail a cab. Cathy politely wished him goodbye. She did not hand him her card. Cathy at that point was totally unaware that the next time she would meet Stelios she would be in Cyprus and her life would be in danger.

Chapter 5

Thoughts of Hektor always made Cathy come out in goosebumps. She often discussed her physical reactions to him with her flatmate and best friend Alison. Alison Jowell, plump and good-natured, a teacher whom Cathy had first met as a fellow student at University would always have a sensible explanation.

'I wonder what she would make of the healer?' thought Cathy.

Cathy so far had not mentioned the healer to Alison. In fact, Alison knew very little about Cathy. Cathy preferred it that way. Cathy thought not for the first time how bloody unfortunate it was that the healer had access to all her thoughts, whereby nothing could be concealed. Nobody but absolutely nobody else knew anything about her family.

Cathy realised her mind was wandering. She stared at the white walls in the waiting room and the children's toys on the floor but never any children. People sitting and waiting beside her. She listened hard, concentrating fiercely. Had she missed hearing her name being called? The fog in her mind was especially bad today. A vast distance of shadows, she imagined the circles of hell in Dante's *Inferno* in his *Divine Comedy* to be such a place, in particular one circle of hell for sinners of the flesh. A Carnal Canto, indeed! - oh but how she and Jeremy had laughed about it. Sweet Jeremy with his tousled blonde curls who'd taken her virginity with such tenderness. University seemed such a long time ago. A brief spell where she was happy. But Jeremy had died in a car crash and Cathy had mourned her best mate and lover.

And now she was in love again. Oh fate, as gnarled as an olive tree, but the fruit from this tree - the olive, is life sustaining – Cathy recalled the story of Athena, the Goddess of war and wisdom, among other things and her uncle Poseidon, who were both very fond of a certain city in Greece. Both of them claimed the city and it was decided that the one that could give the finest gift should have it. Leading a procession of citizens, the two gods mounted the Acropolis. Poseidon struck the side of the cliff with his trident and a spring welled up. The people marvelled, but the water was as salty as Poseidon's sea and it was not very useful. Athena's gift was an olive tree, which was better because it gave the people food, oil and wood. Athena named her city Athens.

Is my fate to be of such twisted bark as the olive tree, thought Cathy, as the hair on her arms stood on end with a sudden insight, and what of the fruit? Cathy bit her lip- she knew that in her case, the fruit was forbidden. 'Don't think of that now, don't think of the guilt' Cathy said to herself. She looked at her watch. It was twelve-thirty.

I will be cutting things a bit fine. The appointment at the University is at two, she thought to herself.

She looked around at the other people waiting to be seen. A man stared back at her intently. He was swarthy and bearded. Cathy looked away. She was used to men looking at her. She usually ignored them. 'I must ask how long this is going to take. I'll give it another five minutes.' The receptionists kept eyeing her curiously. She smiled at them tiredly, then stared ahead.

God she hadn't slept much again. The healer had been talking to her all through the night. For many nights now he had visited her, probing, dissecting, questioning hour after hour any choice bit of information that could be garnered from her mind. Cathy had had to fight with all her mind not to think of anything, to keep her mind a blank. Sometimes she succeeded. Sometimes she didn't. Then he would seize on the most trivial thing and probe as to her reasons for her actions. The whole process was exhausting.

Cathy shivered in the clinical atmosphere. Her mind had been going through a whirlpool for the last half-hour whilst waiting for the appointment. Her past laid bare with the healer asking so many questions. She was glad he had left. She deliberately got to her feet. She must stop the memories. She would be physically ill if she did not. The fog, induced by the healer's presence, was clearing from her brain. Had he hypnotised her?

She glanced at her watch. The waiting was interminable. She thought if her name wasn't called in the next five minutes, she would have to leave and reschedule the appointment. Ten minutes later, she approached the girls at the desk with the intention of doing just that when the man who had been staring at her earlier barged past her. He looked threatening as he stared at her but he was only making his way to the gent's toilet. The healer's last words of interference rang in Cathy's brain. Cathy tensed. Something was not right. Was she being fanciful or did she have the power of clairvoyancy as the healer said?

The girl at the desk raised her eyebrows, Fran Mitchell her badge said. Cathy caught the words she said to her co-worker. 'That's the seventh time in half an hour he's been to the loo. He seems distressed.'

Cathy relaxed. Poor chap, Cathy thought, He probably has a compulsive disorder to wash his hands or something.

The dark-skinned man who had brushed past Cathy a few seconds earlier was Mehmet, the trainee. He locked the door of the gent's toilet and spoke very softly into his mobile phone. The occupant of the beaten up Volkswagen in the car park, just outside, listened to the soft voice. He had been tuning into the conversation within the building on his specially equipped radio. He now said in crisp tones, 'You will arouse suspicion checking in so often.'

'Not in this place' was the soft answer.

'It may take another hour for her to be seen. How is Fatima getting on with checking on Xanthis?'

The occupant of the Volkswagen thumped his fist on the steering wheel. He was big and burly. He said 'you stupid bastard, don't say anything else on this frequency. We will discuss the matter back at the flat. Wait a minute I can see her at the door now. She is not waiting. She is leaving. I'll take it from here'

Cathy had got fed-up with the waiting. She had rescheduled her appointment. She left the building walking quickly and gracefully. She didn't want to be late for the interview today. Cathy hoped to get the job of teaching Ancient Greek to raw beginners, year 1 students of Classics, at the University. It was an hour's daily slot and was regular work, she could always fit in her other clients around that time. Cathy checked her watch. She had half an hour before the interview. The drive there would take ten minutes. She had time now to get a drink and a sandwich, she spotted a café and went inside.

The burly man following her watched her enter the café and take a seat by the window. 'All the better to see you my dear', he said aloud.

He believed she was totally unaware of his presence as she was unaware that the telephone in her apartment was tapped and of the highly-sensitive surveillance equipment that monitored every word spoken in the flat. The two men and one woman located in the building opposite compiled the day's recordings, made an assessment and sent it on to Istanbul. They had hacked into the feed of the CCTV cameras in the street outside and the entrance to the building was highlighted nicely. The watching team could see all who entered and left the building. The windows of the flat they were currently occupying were directly opposite Cathy's and afforded enough of a view to determine most of Cathy's movements.

Abdullah, the burly individual, looked at Cathy and smiled grimly to himself as he thought, not for the first time, how unobservant most people were. This one is particularly naive. Beautiful but naive - although sometimes he wondered if she had an inkling of his presence- she would turn her head unexpectedly when he was on her trail and stare straight at him. She never voiced her suspicions aloud though and he should know, as he was privy to most of her conversations, thanks to the surveillance the team employed.

Abdullah shrugged and thought in the six months she had been watched, the girl had had no contact with the target. Yet Turkey had been convinced that they were on the right track. They had had a man from Kyrenia, Northern Cyprus, from his, Abdullah's neck of the woods, on the job during the girl's last visit, six months ago to the south of the island of Cyprus. Just thinking of Cyprus, Abdullah's home - such an ancient land and the etymology of the name Cyprus – Abdullah's mind wandered and he considered which variation of the word he liked best. Was it Cyprus of the henna plant (kypros plant) or copper (cuprum) mining that had existed on the island. Abdullah liked the one suggestion that it comes from the Greek word for the Mediterranean Cypress tree.

Abdullah thought, 'I come from such a country where the Assyrians and the Persians, the Romans and the Venetians all left their mark in ancient times and more recently the Ottoman Turks, his, Abdullah's ancestors.....'

Abdullah saw Cathy talking to the waitress which brought Abdullah's mind back to the subject. He recalled it was the Kyrenian, their man from Northern Cyprus, the man who had tailed Cathy on her last visit, who had assured them that although he had no concrete proof of a liaison at that time between Burkert and the target, constant surveillance of the girl would result in a connection being established.

The man who now watched Cathy thought, with a quickly stifled pang of homesickness, of his hometown, Kyrenia in Northern Cyprus. He reflected how access to the south of the island was made easier, since the gates were opened at the green line that defined the borders between the north and the south of Cyprus.

'Two factions- we were brothers living in harmony- Greek and Turkish, main inhabitants of our beautiful country.'

Abdullah shook his head in woe at the thought that for twenty-nine years Cyprus had been a divided country. Ever since the Turkish invasion of 1974 - an invasion that was condemned worldwide. The South of Cyprus became inhabited by the Greek Cypriots whilst the North by the Turkish Cypriots. Turkey controlled the North and was the only country to recognise the government of the North. With no co-operation or recognition from the rest of the world, Northern Cyprus felt increasingly isolated.

But now, thought Abdullah NOW we have a chance. A referendum was to be held on April 24 2004 on re-unification of the North and the South. The Turkish Cypriots wanted to change their lives. They wanted to be one country. They had suffered isolation since 1974 as they had had no international recognition. Having suffered hardship and deprivation they had watched their Greek counterparts with envy, as in the South, tourism had taken off in a big way and the Greeks had prospered. Abdullah now thanked Allah for the man, his employer, who would prove to be a hero to Turkey and Northern Cyprus. The great Nasr Al-din.

A formidable man, rich and powerful. Abdullah knew some of the stories that circulated about the man. Nobody knew the actual truth. Abdullah recollected the one that he had heard recently that Al-din had arrived on mainland Turkey with little or nothing, a mere boy of 18, how he had worked hard and was lucky to have got employment in the Persian Gulf. There in the desert kingdom of Saudi Arabia, he worked on the construction of a Palace for one of the ruling family.

Abdullah thought the story got a bit far-fetched from then on for not only was Al-din reputed to have saved the life of the sheik from falling masonry but the sheik had rewarded him by giving him a large sum of money. Al-din had used the money to buy the construction company and that's how he had got started on the road to money and power! Masallah! (Wonderful!)

Abdullah knew that Al-din had over the years acquired a vast portfolio of property and hotels and now had major interests in Turkey's natural resources. Rumour had it that he had ambitions for the new project- the Nabucco pipeline.

This is the man Abdullah knew with blind conviction who would ensure that Turkey would succeed in its application to join the EU. So far their application had been rejected mainly because Cyprus was a divided island. Turkey's invasion and continued control of the North of Cyprus was the major stumbling block.

But the re-unification of the north and south of Cyprus was just a referendum away. A UN backed referendum with the Press referring to the proposed plan for re-unification as 'The Annan Plan' in recognition of the efforts of the head of the UN, Kofi Annan. The North vote was an assured 'yes' –Turkey would orchestrate that. Once the North and South were re-united, Turkey's access to the European Union would be a mere formality.

Abdullah remembered his training in Turkey where he had spent a year learning surveillance and counterintelligence techniques - the political school he had attended was a compulsory part of the training course. In class, with a chosen few, he had studied the reality of the political situation today in Turkey and the fact that two superpowers, America and Britain, were and still are in great rivalry over Turkey, each with a strong influence on the Turkish political scene.

The US and the Brits needed the focus to be moved from Russia with its dominance over gas and oil, as rumours were abounding that Putin, the President of Russia, was setting events in motion to ensure Russia had a stranglehold on gas and oil. The Nabucco pipeline going through Turkey would ensure that Europe would have an alternative to Russian dominance over energy sources. Besides, Turkey was the gateway by which Britain and the US could influence Middle-Eastern politics.

Abdullah thought, I thank God we have Britain and America rooting for us- powerful forces indeed! Their spy-networks must be buzzing in Cyprus with such major events looming. If Greek Cyprus rejects the Referendum, these powerful forces were going to be seriously displeased.

That could happen for there was a fly in the ointment.

Abdullah now felt a sense of blind rage when he thought of the reason everything may not be going according to plan. One bastard, he thought, to incite a nation. The North required a positive vote from the

Greek side BUT.. There were rumblings that not all the Greek Cypriots were in favour of voting yes. One man seemed to be the loudest – his voice was urging negativity - Hektor Xanthis. His control of the local newspapers and television stations ensured that the plan on reunification was being scrutinised minutely and in a lot of cases found wanting.

Abdullah knew that for his boss in Turkey, the great Nasr Al-din, a lot was riding on the Greeks voting 'yes' in favour of the Annan plan. The Greeks, Al-din would repeat incessantly, must be persuaded to see things Ankara's way.

By fair means or foul.

'Which brings me to this moment – here in this cold, alien landscape, far from friends and family, to why I am watching the fair Cathy, thought Abdullah, forcing back his anger and pursing his lips in resolution. They were expecting results, his bosses back in Turkey. This was his last shot. Everything else had failed. He had even increased surveillance to the maximum but – nothing! All they had managed to piece together over the past weeks was just a lot of crap about some healer and psychic phenomena!

'She is the channel through which we could influence Xanthis, I am convinced of it,' thought Abdullah, even though the trail is very faint at the moment. 'I'll phone in my report, perhaps there will be something useful that will come to light in her conversations with Mallard' he thought. He watched her toss back the long black hair as she sat by the window of the café and made the call.

Chapter 6

Abdullah switched his phone off and watched Cathy get into her old mini. He ran across to where his car was parked and followed at a safe distance. Earlier Fatima had said the GPS system was not working today so he had to physically do the legwork of trailing Cathy. He switched on his specially tuned radio to pick up any conversations she might have in the car on her mobile phone. Some clue as to her plans for the rest of the day. Otherwise, he Abdullah would be following blind. She appeared to be parking and getting out. Was she headed for the university? Yes, she was. The name outside the building was the Classics Department. It would be a simple matter to find out who Cathy Burkert had an appointment with today at the University's Classics department. Abdullah made the call. The receptionist proved very helpful.

An hour later as he watched her walk towards her car, he noticed an air of jauntiness about her. He switched on the radio, as she seated herself behind the wheel, and realised she was making a call. To his delight it was on speakerphone. Saved a lot of legwork, he thought.

'Mum, how are you?", he heard her say.

Abdullah pressed the button to record. He would analyse it later. Following her at a safe distance he realised that she was heading back to her flat.

'Good' he thought 'the other team can take over.' Half an hour later, Abdullah played back the tape of her conversation earlier in the car.

'Allah o Akbar' he said 'at last a breakthrough. So, Missy, you are soon to be close to my hunting ground.' He picked up the phone and spoke to his boss, the icy Russian.

'She is heading for Cyprus. In two weeks. Naturally we will be hot on her trail. Apparently rare papyri has been discovered, relating to Homer. It could shake up the world of Classical literature – something to do with proof that Homer was definitively the author of the *Iliad* and the *Odyssey*. A great find for the boffins. Cathy Burkert is part of a three man team asked to go along from the University to assist in the translation and analysis. Apparently she got lucky. The person scheduled to go just had a heart attack, and there is no one else free at such short notice. But Igor, get this, she told her mother she hoped to have a bit of free time to see her friend in Cyprus. No she didn't mention names. Hopefully, the friend in question is our pigeon.'

The next few days were very busy for Cathy. She had a lot to get organised before she left for Cyprus. Cathy fitted in meetings at the University with the professor who would be leading the team, Malcolm Grant and his assistant, Tessa Banks whilst doing her normal schedule of interpreting. Her regular clients, rich students who were completing their Phd's (Doctorates) and needed help with Greek and Italian translations were easy to reschedule whilst she was away. She informed the embassies, her other source of income that she would be away for a couple of weeks. In the midst of mentally ticking off her checklist of all the things that had to be done, Cathy, in her bedroom packing, looked in the mirror and saw the healer watching her. Her heart sank.

'Who had let him in? Not tonight,' she thought, 'I'm too tired.'

Not after last night. He had been by her side for a rigorous two hours and afterward she had difficulty drifting off to sleep. Horrid memories swirling around in her brain, she recalled some of the conversation last night. She felt raw, bloody when she thought of his words.

'Did your brother, Mark, rape you? Tell me what happened, Cathy. I want to know every detail, every single moment of your shame'

Over and over he asked the question. Cathy would not answer.

She had said nothing but she had not been able to stop the memories. She had squirmed mentally and physically and felt the need to lie on the bed in a foetal position with the covers drawn tightly around her, cocooning her.

The healer persisted with the questions. 'What happened? I have to know.'

She started crying. 'He did not rape me' she said quietly 'He touched me'

'Where did he touch you?'

'On my breasts'

'Where else, Cathy?

'Nowhere'

'Are you sure?'

'Yes. Yes.' Her mind wandered back. *She was a child again. Barely thirteen with the promise of beauty already apparent. She had started menstruating. Her mother reticent about sexual matters and body functions did not explain. Cathy barely understood the lessons at school about birth and the sexual act. One night in the bedroom she shared with her sister, she remembered coming out of a deep sleep to feel a presence above her. Hands on her breasts.*

She said to the healer, 'Mark used to sneak up at night when everyone was asleep and I used to wake up with him looming over the bed with his hands on me. It was terrifying.'

'Why didn't you tell your parents?'

'I did but they wouldn't believe me'

'Did you feel terrible that you were not believed?'

'Yes,' tears rolling down her cheek at the memory, 'I didn't know whom to turn to. I was helpless'

'How long did it carry on for?' 'A few weeks until I...' The healer watched her, his eyes looked flinty. 'What stopped him Cathy?'

'I stopped him. I hid a knife under my pillow and the next time Mark came to the bed I threatened him with it. He didn't do it again' she said quietly.

'Did you feel it was your fault? Did you feel you were a bad person?'

'Yes I did. I felt bad- dirty!' She shifted restlessly to stop remembering any more.

The healer watched her avidly. 'What did you do Cathy to stop feeling like a bad person? A sinner? You with your Catholic upbringing. The guilt must have eaten away at you. Did you do something good or did you do something bad?'

'No, no, don't', pleaded Cathy, 'don't ask me any more'

The healer looked away. He said 'Okay, I would say no more tonight as you have taken a giant step forward trusting me about your brother- but my sweet, I'm agog to hear the rest of the family diatribe. Now just sit down. There you are'. He took her hand, 'tell me about your father's business-what happened next? By the way, have you told anyone outside your parents about Mark?'

Cathy shook her head. 'No, I couldn't. Too ashamed' she whispered.

'Yes I can see that.... ummm and Cathy dearest you were a mere child- nothing to feel guilty about but I think to overcome your guilt, you did something bad, something you consider very bad. Now let's talk about your childhood.

Cathy was starting to feel spaced out again. The healer reminded her that she was now nine years old and her father's business dominated her life. *She remembered her ninth birthday and Dad wasn't there. He was too busy setting up the factory. Cathy remembered her mother Lucia had explained when Cathy was eighteen. Simon apparently had started full of confidence. He was in partnership with the Dutch and the money they contributed went into purchasing the heavy-duty machinery for the factory. All Simon needed was a bank loan for his running costs. The loan from the bank would cover the purchase of the essential ingredients and employ staff. In fact, it would keep them going for the next year until profits were realised.*

Any day now, Simon thought and the factory will be a going concern. In the meantime he had to maintain the house and grounds and the same social whirl. That's why he needed investors. Simon held many a grand party in his home to woo his investors. He would offer them shares in the company. Simon would take them to see the factory. These businessmen were impressed with the size of the building which was fully equipped with all the latest technology for the start of production. They felt flattered to be included in the deal. So they paid up. Simon didn't ask for much. A few thousands at a time. At that stage, Simon had no intention of cheating them. He would repay them with handsome dividends once business was under way.

'So he used the money from the investors to fund his living costs. Well, well. He must have been pretty sure of the bank paying up' said the healer.

Cathy whispered, 'You see, he wasn't careful with the money. I think it was because of his upbringing in the orphanage where he had to subsist on very little. It made him spend recklessly the money he received as investments.'

For Simon lived lavishly. They ate the best food at home and dined in the best restaurants – the whole family. Simon was expansive in those days. The children had few beatings. Many an evening, Cathy would sit in her mother's bedroom and watch her getting dressed for a party, either at their home, where the children were allowed downstairs for a little while or at her parents' friends and business associates. Cathy thought her mother looked beautiful. Warm toffee Taffeta and old lace – Cathy loved seeing her mother in that particular dress.

Sitting in her living-room with the healer beside her, the words tumbled out of Cathy. She felt the need to confess all to the healer, hoping for absolution, perhaps.

All about the banks not touching Simon's loan application. They smelled a rotting corpse and would not touch it. He was forced to re-mortgage the house. Simon with the money carried on living the high life.

A year later, and still trying to raise finance for the factory, his money from the house ran out. He had no income. The Dutch sued Simon for non-payment of the loan. Simon's investors from his business contacts started to demand their money back. The word had spread that he was a bad investment. More court cases ensued. Simon had to spend many a day attending court. Simon became desperate. He was cruel to Lucia when she heard the news of her father's death. He would say to her,

'Rudolfo has died! Your father has gone and bloody kicked the bucket- can't go to him for a handout, can I? What's more the perfumery is in debt- no inheritance for you there. Your mother blames Rudolfo's death on me- the blasted woman says that I deserted the company thereby alienating their regular custom and

Rudolfo couldn't withstand the pressure. She wants help from me- no bloody fear!' Simon could not go down that road. He turned to his friends and neighbours with the story of the factory, and asked them for loans.

Only, Simon knew there was to be no factory. His friends and acquaintances trusted him absolutely and gave generously from their savings. Simon managed to pay his household bills for the next six months. As whilst the case was being fought in court, Simon still had access to the factory. He would take his friends around it and they had no reason to suspect his intentions. But that source started drying up as well.

With production still not under way after a year, his friends and acquaintances started to ask ever so politely at first as to the reason. Simon charmed them into holding on. He finally had to admit the factory was a non-starter, as the courts had confiscated the *premises and its equipment as payment to the Dutch principals. However, Simon said confidently, they would be paid back as he planned to sell the house. What they didn't know was the banks were foreclosing on the property as Simon could not pay the mortgage. Simon used every excuse in the book to delay his eviction but after six months he accepted the inevitable. The family moved out*

Cathy said softly to the healer, 'I remember Mum during that time.' *Mum was poorly constantly. The tension and worry had made her physically ill. Fiona and Cathy tried to look after her the best they could whilst still adjusting to their surroundings and having to fend for themselves without Leah and the other help. The new council house was very small for all of them and their belongings. They were constantly bumping into each other and Mark, Cathy's older brother showed signs of becoming as vicious as his father.*

He was particularly mean one day to his younger siblings threatening them with his fist. The doorbell rang mid-morning, a small group of friends and neighbours who had given Simon sums of money were outside. One of them had the local newspaper. He waved it at Cathy. 'Your bloody father has cheated us' he said. 'The papers have got hold of it. The whole story is out'

Shame washed over Cathy. 'May I', she stammered nervously. The man shoved the paper at her. Cathy's eyes quickly took in the photograph of her father and the headline 'Local con-man exposed' Her eyes skimmed over the words almost uncomprehending. People's hard-earned savings were lost. Some elderly people were ruined. She threw the paper down and ran into the empty kitchen. She sank to the floor and prayed to God that the nightmare would end. But it had only just begun.

For the rest of that year, Cathy's twelfth, the callers were plenty – people she had known most of her life would call around but they did not want to talk or be pleasant. They would be mostly men, the wives would never show. Daddy would go and see them, he would explain that he had declared himself bankrupt and could not ever repay them, but there would be voices raised in a dreadful anger from the living-room. The house was so small that it was impossible not to hear what was being said. Cathy heard threats, futile talk of court cases, some of them shouted and screamed. Once Cathy felt so ashamed and besmirched by hearing her father repeatedly being called a cheat, she said to herself, 'The neighbours will hear. I can't let that happen'. She ran into the living-room and began shutting all the windows. Cathy never forgot that moment. It was a hot August day, there were five men in the living-room and her father. She tried to creep about shutting the windows without them noticing. The room was too small. They began to shout at Cathy 'Leave the windows open. Let everybody hear how your father who fooled us with all his talk, is a liar and a thief. This man should be behind bars. We want our money back. Leave the bloody windows open I tell you'

Cathy put her hands over her ears to shut the screaming voice out. She said bravely, defiantly, 'I will shut the windows'. The next thing she knew was a strong hand had landed on her jaw and face.

The pain and her father saying, 'Don't touch her'. For once Simon was not the hitter. The man who hit her was uncaring. 'The children are just like their father, wilful. She deserved that'. He left with his friends pushing her father aside. Simon looked shocked. He was staring at the fireplace behind Cathy. He pointed it out to Lucia. The metal screen seemed to *be bending and twisting. Cathy did not notice, she was clutching her jaw in pain.*

Cathy's jaw was so swollen that she couldn't leave the house for two days after. But more importantly, Cathy felt as if she had the stuffing knocked out of her. For years she had been slapped around, beaten with a cane and with a belt by her father - but the fact that another man could hit her as well, a stranger, to whom she had done nothing. Deep down Cathy believed that she deserved the physical abuse. She was naughty, that's why she got beatings. Daddy was justified in hitting her but this other man - hitting someone else is wrong she thought. Nothing but nothing can make up for the humiliation of being hit in the face. The blow on the face takes away your belief in yourself. I will not let him win. That horrid man. I must not cry. If I never give them the satisfaction of crying then I will have won. Cathy did not cry. Not for a long time.

The healer had looked at her and soothed her with soft words. He had left shortly after and Cathy had felt emotionally steamrolled.

Cathy dragged her thoughts back with a shudder and looked at him now. Here he was again smiling at her. She had given him the key to come and go as he pleased and now, just for an instant, she felt a pang of regret.

She said, 'I can't do this. Not tonight. I'm too tired.'

'So am I, my beauty. I've had a bloody long day at the surgery. You never ask me about my life, Missy. Aren't you interested?'

'I know about your life,' she said. Two years ago when she had first read one of his books about healing she had gone onto the web to find out more about him.

She said, 'I know that you were born with special energy and that you assisted in lab. experiments with the great scientists to convert matter with your energy.

Their findings led to cures and voila you became famous. That was ten years ago. You lived the high life for the first five, drinking and partying but one day five years ago on a remote hillside in some inaccessible place, you decided to change your life. You decided to use that energy to heal people directly. People who have tried every other cure and have no hope come to you. Your success rate is high. So now you are even more famous and more in demand. You are practically a household name with non-medical healing.'

Cathy paused. 'I haven't asked you about your life' she added reluctantly and almost inaudibly, 'because I didn't think I was important enough for you to share news of your life with me.'

'Whoops' he said, 'just as I think I've laid Cathy Burkert bare, she appears self-effacing. Where's your sassiness? I bet it takes something special to walk into an interview room for one little job and then convince your employers that you are the perfect person to unravel Homer's genius. Didn't think I knew about that, did you?

My dear I am privy to all your thoughts. Even when I am away from you. We share this special bond. We are telekinetic and telepathic. Just the two of us in the whole world. No-one else knows. Are you aware how special we are? How utterly privileged! Everything you think registers in my head and that is the problem. I can't have all your Greek and Italian lessons and other random thoughts interfere with my thinking. So I have taken care of the matter.

He stared at her his eyes hard and probing, his tone had an edge to it, he said ever so softly, 'Young lady, did you just think the word TELEPATHY should be- 'TELE-PATHETIC- ? Not funny indeed! Let me put a question to you. Tell me the truth now. You know I have access to every thought. Yes, my dear, even when you consider whether it's time to have your tampax changed.' He looked at Cathy's red face.

Cathy was squirming, 'It's not true. I can't bear for him to know every thought. How am I going to cope? I can't *not* think!'

The healer said, 'Now, now, no need to panic. Think of me as a doctor. By the way, have you ever had any thoughts of mine enter your head?'

Cathy stared at him her eyes round. She felt profoundly shocked. She sat down and whispered 'You told me I was a telepathist. You put a name to something that I have always been able to do and therefore taken for granted- Random thoughts and an impression of a person does enter my mind and later these persons -friends and family, work colleagues confirm the impressions I get in advance- but I don't believe I have received your thoughts in my head, to answer the question. Moreover, I don't believe that you know everything I think. Nobody can have access to another person's mind. It's not humanly possible.'

He laughed 'My innocent little one. Ok. I see no reason why I can't tell you something about all of this. I'm going to tell you about a certain professor who conducted an experiment with his wife to prove that such a connection could be established. He implanted a tiny little gizmo to her wrist and then hooked her up to a computer. Do you want to hear the rest?

She shook her head. She was scared and panicking. Every thought? What if he found out about….don't think.. stop it. Stop it now.'

He looked at her suspiciously. 'Hmmm… As I was saying, the professor needed a machine and implants to aid telepathy but you and I need no such medium. We can communicate naturally but I have had to ensure that every stray thought of yours- inane stuff like what to wear for the day down to your sexual urges of the moment does not register in my head and disturb my own thought process. I have invented a special machine to divert your thoughts when I am busy.

'It's not true, I don't believe you', Cathy said desperately nearly in tears. 'I'm not listening to any more. I want you to leave. Please go.'

'My selfish little beauty - But you have to hear it. It comes with the territory. I listen to your deepest darkest secrets and attempt to heal all your torments and in exchange I have access to all your thoughts. Why? He paused and considered 'Call it payment. I'm not entirely altruistic you know, I've got my own agenda. Consider it research for a book I intend to write or maybe, just maybe I think what the two of us have is so precious that I would go to any lengths to discover everything about you. He looked harshly at her, 'You don't see that do you? You don't even begin to understand what we have. I have to heal you before you can commit to me. And one day I promise you, you will!'

Cathy stared at him. She said, 'You have to go. I have to be up early'.

He ignored her and continued, 'Cathy I have travelled the world, I have met all sorts of people from princesses, oil sheiks to the humblest, poorest people, people who have experienced tremendous suffering and pain and I have tried to heal them. Mostly I've had success. I realised some time ago that healing was the answer, helping people with the gifts I have been given. It's my calling, my raison d'etre. Do you understand Cathy Burkert? I am a kind man. But with you I want to be cruel. I want to turn you inside out, empty each and every little corner of that mind of yours, uncover every secret and I shall find out, all of it. I am planning to take some time off…'.

Cathy interrupted him. She had to know. Her voice was croaky. She made an effort to speak strongly, 'I understand that we are telepathists and we communicate with each other – you've told me often enough! But the machine you mentioned, to divert my thoughts. Is this true? How can you do such a thing? Answer me, Matt' said Cathy desperately

He said 'Yes to all of the above- Thank God I am getting through. I shall tell you. I got in touch with some old mates, scientists who I have worked with in the past and having given me some basic ideas along with some basic equipment, I set about it. I won't bore you with the technical details. Suffice it to say it has a lot to do with electromagnetism. Basically your thoughts bounce onto this machine rather than into my head. The machine is attached to a computer which stores and prints out your thoughts in words all day and all night. Yes. Every thought. Dreams are something I haven't managed to analyse but technology is advancing all the time. So you can never lie to me sweet Cathy.

All I have to do when I am busy is merely to switch on the machine and check from time to time on the printouts.

Hearing his words, Cathy thought 'I must think in Italian.'

The healer laughed, 'Language decoders have been installed. Whatever language you think in the printouts are in beautiful Queens English. I'm currently working on the concept of introducing several of my machines in different corners of the globe, hooking them up to satellites and creating thought transference between peoples, using your natural abilities as a conduit. We could travel the world- you and I. Conduct thought transference between people who are in need of help. I am a healer and I believe you with your innocence and your senses honed to a high degree – (my input will take them sky-high), you can help me to heal people. No words, no speech, no physical presence required. Just your mind!

Cathy, people find it really difficult to say things out loud in person, for fear of ridicule or recrimination sometimes even incarceration. But thinking is not a crime. Cathy, imagine how criminals could be helped by changing their thought processes. Your ability to reason things out, to help them understand where they have gone wrong, not in speech - just thoughts bouncing into their minds before they commit their evil thoughts into action. Before they rob, maim, murder. You have the ability to convert their thinking.

Yes Cathy I have been hesitant to tell you until now. But I must- the time has come for you to take centre-stage. My dear, that is why with my background I am so enamoured of you. I have found my alter-ego. You have the ability not just for thought transference but the one ingredient that is essential to healing. You have developed an extreme sensitivity to people. That is why you could help people. You could do that. You could save them. Because you don't need to be hooked up to any machine. You are a natural. So am I. The only two in the world.

We need technology to assist us, only to get to the minds of others- hence the need to set up a machine. Together our natural electrical energy will do the deed – remotely influence other minds.

Do I detect doubt in you? Cathy it is essential you believe that it takes the both of our combined energy to make the machine work. I have stored an imprint of my electrical energy on a computer chip, which is accessed via the machine- therefore no physical presence required!

I can't personally be 'The Conduit,' he said, placing due emphasis on the word, 'but I will help and guide you. Do you agree, my sweet Cathy? I could set up the whole operation, transfer the machine or machines in a week, to different locations and contact people to try and share their thoughts with you – registered psychopaths, paedophiles, - He held his hands up and said 'so many in need. I could have that up and running within the next couple of weeks, when you are in Cyprus. Think about it.' He looked at Cathy's desperate face.

'Alright I'm going. He was at the door. 'Oh if you are tempted to tell anybody about this um communication, don't. It's highly secret. For a very good reason. You see, the machine I invented not only registers your thoughts – it can also input information into your mind. That's how I plan to guide you. With my influence you would know exactly what to think and say. But we wouldn't want just anybody to know that would we? Think of how they could input their thoughts and wishes and could get you to do things unconscious of your own desire to do so.

No, Cathy I'm not a villain,' he second-guessed her, 'The only reason for me prompting a thought or two in your mind is for the greater good- to help people. However, If the machine falls into the wrong hands you could be used as a very different conduit, oh – let's say – you could be persuaded to carry drugs or for murder or getting to someone who is in power.'

'You're panicking, Cathy, I can see your face. I know what you're thinking. I will say no more. Don't even think of going to the police. Because you would, wouldn't you? Shop me? The police will never believe you. I know you will try though. Go ahead.' He stood up. 'I'm off now. Enjoy Cyprus. Who knows, perhaps you'll miss me and send for me. I'll hotfoot it to the ends of the world for you'

In the flat opposite the tapes kept running. Fatima had turned the sound off whilst she watched television in the next room. She would check on them in the next hour. She must check to see if there had been any visitors to Miss Burkert's flat. She played back the tape on the CCTV feed to the entrance of the building. The plump flatmate had left earlier, no doubt on the razz. Fatima would never understand how these English girls could dress so revealingly. Her orthodox Muslim background would never permit her to wear anything that showed off her cleavage let alone leave her arms bare. Orospu (bitch), she thought, I feel they deserve all the trouble they get. She switched the tape off. No visitors by the front anyway. They had not bothered to cover the back as they reasoned that Cathy was totally unaware of their presence so therefore would not be likely to get anybody coming in from the back entrance. Besides the windows were open and she could look directly into the flat opposite. No sign of anything out of the ordinary there. Good. 'I will just do a quick check on the audio tapes from the flat'

To her surprise, there was a man's voice. Fatima had not seen anyone there. He must have been in the bedroom, sneaking in from the back entrance. A camera would have to be installed in the bedroom. Burkert with a man in the bedroom, thought Fatima, that's unusual. Her eyes glowed as she heard the conversation on the tape. She expected a bonus this year, a hefty one. She e-mailed her report in matter of fact tones not conveying any of the excitement she felt. She worked long into the night doing research on Mr. Matt Mallard. She knew what the next instruction would be from Istanbul and she had made sure she was ready for it.

Chapter 7

Abdullah had his instructions. He was to try and install listening devices in Xanthis offices here in London. He called his mate to arrange pick-up. He would have to be very, very careful.

2 pm and Abdullah now dressed in blue overalls with Masons Removal Company emblazoned on the back entered the building close to London's Chinatown. He was later than expected. Traffic in Oxford Street had been at its usual manic pace with the incessant traffic lights – an obstacle race of red, green and amber and surging humanity holding him up.

He looked down at his clipboard pretending to make notes with his pen as he passed two beautifully dressed girls coming out of the lift. The lift shot up to the fourth floor. The receptionist was middle-aged of Asian origin. He told her that he had been sent by the removal company to take away the defunct air-conditioning unit in the storage room.

Fatima back at HQ had set the scene. She had called, touting for custom as Masons, the removal company and had been told about the A/c unit that had been lying about for years. The office was expanding and the extra room was needed. The company would be jolly glad to have the thing removed.

Abdullah followed the receptionist and chatted with her pleasantly. She told him how the big boss from Cyprus was expected at any time. His office was adjacent to the store. The unit was big and bulky. Abdullah needed room to manoeuvre it into the narrow corridor. Would she mind if he left the boss' door ajar to allow ease of movement? She agreed and set off back to the ringing telephone on her desk.

Abdullah eased his weight behind the old-fashioned steel unit. He lifted it out through the store room door and wedged it in the open doorway of the adjacent office. He lifted his leg to climb over it to enter the office feeling for the bugs in his pocket. The office was furnished elegantly- black leather and chrome but was definitely a working office. Papers in overflowing trays strewn across the desk. Abdullah felt the same old rush of adrenaline when he was on a job- he lifted the telephone and started to take the instrument to pieces.

Black eyes looked at the man. The features of the man standing by his phone looked Cypriot thought Hektor as he peered around the corner of the door to his office. Something was blocking the doorway. He said loudly, 'What can I do for you?'

The man started visibly- He shoved the phone out of sight under some of the papers and said, 'Just trying to call for help. That thing, indicating the A/C unit, seems to be stuck fast.'

Hektor, the hair on his arms raised, looked suspiciously at the man. He said in Greek, 'Where do you come from?'

Abdullah said, 'Sorry don't understand the language, mate'

Hektor still persisted. He repeated in English. 'Where do you come from?'

'Mason's Removal Company' said Abdullah bending to lift the heavy weight of the unit. Hektor was forced to back away as the man picked up the unit and moved towards him. His gaze fell to the trouser pocket of the man as he passed him. There were wires poking out, practically falling out of the pocket.

Abdullah his back breaking from the load, put the unit down and waited for the lift. Hektor followed him and said, ' You're going to lose your ---Headphones? What is it? The man looked strange thought Hektor. For one thing he was sweating heavily. Secondly there was naked aggression in the man's dark eyes. Hektor sensed hatred. Hektor needed to detain him to find out why. He instantly decided against calling for an assistant.

Hektor said, 'Listen you look as if you need a glass of water. Let me get you one.' Hektor put a detaining hand on the man's arm. The man moved swiftly jerking his hand away. He turned towards the stairs. He said, 'I'm fine- just going to leave this unit here and come back with some help. Be back in an hour'

Abdullah ran down the four flights of stairs and wiped his leaking forehead on his sleeve. Bastard, he said, what a bastard- nearly had the job done. He walked quickly to his car and drove off with the ice cold hatred starting to solidify within him. One more job to do.

Matt Mallard felt a touch of self-hatred as looked at his computer screen. The email he had just opened confirmed details of delivery times. His machine was nearly ready to go and he should be pleased that all his painstaking plans over many months were finally in place but he was concerned. Cathy was going to have to go under the influence, (as he liked to call it) it was really a form of mild hypnosis he induced in his patients when he conducted certain healing therapies- he also knew the machine, once enhanced, would cause a benumbing effect. The combination of the two, was going to exhaust him. Cathy would, he knew, be similarly affected. He set his jaw and a determined look crossed his face.

'All for the greater good' he said aloud. He felt a renewed sense of vigour just thinking of the path ahead. A feeling of emptiness had pervaded his life of late, a restlessness plaguing him- Cathy was the answer- the end of my quest for the holy grail! People in need connected through the electronic sixth sense that he had spent months developing.

A noise disturbed his musing. He wandered to the window and looked out onto the garden. Mallard's surgery was housed in a thatched cottage overlooking Harpenden Common. He lived there on his own, his wife having died five years previously. He was an attractive man and his electrical energy created a physical response within women so he was never short of a female companion.

He had come across Cathy quite by accident. He remembered the party had been in full swing when he had got there. The house he had been invited to was too blue, he recalled. His hostess was the decor's culprit, he guessed, as her surroundings echoed her dress of silver and blue. A long-absent emotional kick in his gut brought a sudden insight. Something or someone so intrinsic to his life was a heartbeat away. His eyes were drawn to a young girl amongst the crowd, black hair flowing dressed in peach chiffon, tightly swathed. She looked at him and walked toward him. Cathy Burkert. He could read her mind.

The van pulled up to the door of Mallard's cottage. Abdullah in the same blue overalls he had been wearing earlier, knocked on the door. Mallard presumably was out as nobody answered the knock or the doorbell as Abdullah depressed the button. The right side of the house was sheltered by a tall hedge. The back door was located there. Abdullah punched a hole in the glass and the key on the inside of the door turned easily giving him access.

Polished wood floors, dark antique furniture and oriental rugs decorated the hallway. There were three doors leading off. Abdullah found the door to the study and his gaze swept narrow eyed around the shelves groaning with books and framed photographs. Mallard knew some important people. He moved to the desk and looked through the papers for anything useful. A machine on the desk caught his eye. It had several switches and was attached to a printer.

Abdullah pressed the main switch on the machine but nothing happened. He took a photograph of it on his mobile phone, sent it on to Igor in Istanbul. Abdullah decided to make another attempt today at planting a listening device in the phone. This time he was successful. He suddenly caught sight of Cyrillic Greek script on a letter in the neatly stacked tray. He picked it up and read it through. A priest's confession. Abdullah felt as though he had struck gold. He let himself out of the house, quietly.

The priest stroked his long beard as he waited to be served his lunch. The meal was sparse as the priest's dietary needs were simple. Beans and bread with salad and some yoghurt to follow. Papa Spiro Antoniou in fact did not feel like food at all. His mind and body seemed weighted down. The burden was sometimes too great.

Mallard had been in touch after many years. As a young man he had met Mallard who was of a similar age. Mallard had been meditating in a monastery in a remote area of the Troodos mountains and Papa Spiro was just undertaking his religious studies. They had met and spoken long into the night of personal spiritual goals and reinvention. Now there was the matter of this girl, Mallard had petitioned his advice.

Papa Spiro was an unusual man, an omniscient, of the same ilk as Mallard and Cathy Burkert. He'd written and supported Mallard's use of the machine on Cathy. He would have done the same, he said in collusion. Besides, Mallard's plea for approbation coincided with his, Papa Spiro's need to use such a machine.

Lately, Papa Spiro had felt the need for turning his life full circle. So many people would benefit. Yes, the machine to control another's thought process would do very well- very well indeed. Especially beneficial to the Greek Cypriots.

The Greek Cypriots were tumbling into a vortex. They were selling their birthright if they voted yes in the referendum. Their land which by virtue of ancestry and Hellenic identity was theirs alone. The word in chosen circles in the church hierarchy was that Papa Spiro knew the man who would destroy Cyprus.

A face in a dream, words laying on his semi-conscious mind, all pointed to impending doom. Papa Spiro became racked with his own sense of the scale of events, then one day he picked up his morning newspaper and recognised his adversary. This was the man who was going to bring Cyprus down. He knew this with absolute certainty. The name was Al-din and Matt's machine would be used to thwart him!

Papa Spiro decided he needed to bring the Americans into the equation.

Chapter 8

Close to Papa Spiro's part of the world, later that day from his eyrie in his tall tower block in Istanbul, in the north-west of Turkey, Nasr Al-din, looked out on the panoramic view of the Bosphorus and barked into the phone. He banged the receiver down. The man who came in through the door caught the full brunt of the vicious look that had been directed a second previously at the newspaper on the desk. 'Have you seen this?' questioned Nasr harshly. 'Xanthis pictured with the President of Cyprus. Yesterday it was with the Minister of Defence. Last week there were pictures of him with two other ministers. I tell you he is lobbying them for support. He is promoting the 'no' vote. It is imperative to Turkey and to me that Southern Cyprus agrees to the Annan plan. 'A 'yes' vote' will ensure that Turkey joins the EU. Igor, are you listening?'

The man standing across from him had the distinctive features of his father's race especially the long nose along with the ice-cold blue eyes, Igor Ahronian who was head of Nasr's security. He listened to the harsh tones, he thought, 'Here he goes again!' He had heard Nasr repeat the same sentences over and over again recently.

'He's going to tell me all about the pipeline in a minute' Igor tuned out and thought about how fortunate he was that Nasr had got in touch with him, a distant cousin on his mother's side during Nasr's visit to Russia all those years ago. Igor had not mentioned his Armenian father to Nasr. The grinding poverty of his, Igor's life had forced him to go to Turkey to work for Nasr but within him burned a resentment kindled by his grandfather's horror stories of the year 1915.

1915 and the agony behind his grandfather's escape and settlement in Russia during the Armenian massacres where the Ottoman Empire, a former-day Turkey caused the systematic slaughter and fatal deportation of hundreds of thousands of Armenians resulting in the utter ruin of their economic and cultural life.

Igor's grandfather, a wealthy merchant had fled in fear of his life. He had lived the life of the poorest peasant in Russia, had married a worker in the factory where he was employed and who spoke his native Turkish. He had died in his prime a bitter and twisted man. That bitterness and anguish had carried through to his only son, Igor's father, who sick and ailing from long hours of physical toil took to his bed, when Igor was very young, ranting and raving of events decades ago, as his life-blood seeped away. And now Igor felt the weight of his grandfather's and father's memories - what a fucked-up inheritance to have!

Igor's mother had not long succeeded his father into the grave and Igor in his teens, had to rely on handouts from the Armenian community to survive. When Igor was growing up he read all about the Armenian genocide - how it is widely acknowledged to have been the first true genocide of the 20th century.

Igor had read with mounting horror how millions of Armenians were exterminated in government organised deportations and massacres in towns and villages strewn across Eastern Anatolia. Under the pretext of disloyalty, the Ottoman government charged that Armenians were siding with the Russian Empire and stipulated that the deportations were born out of the necessity to preserve national security.

Igor grew to be a man with a huge chip on his shoulder. When Nasr had heard of his existence and had sought him out, Igor had seized the opportunity he had been given. He had assiduously courted Nasr's favour, being available at all hours and doing all the dirty little jobs that Nasr asked of him. And it had paid off. His fortunes had risen along with Nasr's and moreover Nasr trusted him absolutely. No doubt because of the family connection. Nasr had no other family as far as Igor knew. And Igor preferred not to know. Just as he preferred that Nasr would never know of Igor's Armenian connection. As far as Nasr was concerned, Igor was his 'lowly Russian cousin' and Igor came to be known as 'The Russian'

'Igor,' Nasr interrupted Igor's train of thought, 'sometimes I wonder if you are aware of what lies at stake here. For me! At the moment Germany is Turkey's major trading partner but I want the whole of Europe. You know I want to have major interests in most of Turkey's natural resources. My sole ambition is to have major stock in the pipeline which will pump 1 million barrels per day of Middle Eastern and Caspian

Sea oil toward Western markets when it becomes fully operational in 2007. We cannot rely solely on Russia. Russia is famous for making unreasonable demands. We have to look towards Europe. My empire needs to go global. It needs EU trading rights. Do you understand?

That bastard Xanthis is using his money and his influence in Cyprus to persuade the public to vote no. His television station hammers out the message daily. Polls are suggesting that he is getting through. There are rumours that he is being groomed to be the next President of the Republic of Cyprus. I know the man. I know him very well. Fortune has indeed favoured him. His acquisition of shipping companies is legendary – do you know how he started? He did a degree on the subject! I am sure his father's money helped to get a step-up.

My government sources tell me that his pet project at the moment is lobbying US support for a resolution denouncing as genocide the deaths of Armenians in the first World War. Deaths and deportations caused by Turkey during its Ottoman Empire days! Well. It's obviously a plot hatched by the Greeks to cause discredit to Turkey. You are looking pale, Igor – get some sun on that white bleached skin of yours!

Personally, Igor I don't give a fuck about the Armenian genocide, my allegiance is to Northern Cyprus, not Turkey, but I am being leant on by Turks in high places. The powers that be here in Turkey, do not want to take any responsibility for the Armenian deaths. I don't mind telling you it's a national affront to admit such an event as the Armenian issue of 1915. That's why Xanthis and the Cypriot Government are using their connections- they want to fuck-up relations between Turkey and the USA- I wouldn't mind betting

Xanthis is contributing to American Armenian coffers, just to destroy relations between Ankara and the US. He will succeed in his endeavours unless he is stopped'. His lips curled in hate. 'That is why you have to do it. Warn him off. Imply there will be consequences'

Igor said, 'It's difficult to get to him. We have been trying both in Cyprus and London but to no avail. His bodyguards are with him all the time. Any attempt at installing listening devices has been thwarted. His rooms are swept every day for just such bugs. We cannot get to him. We have tried every avenue. Just yesterday I had a man in London making a threat to scare Xanthis – you know put the fear of God into him about those tankers of his, but my man had to hightail it out of the country as MI5 started to close in on him. Xanthis has friends in high places. The police protect him. He is a valuable commodity to the country and they take good care of him. However, we believe we have found his Achilles heel. As you know, our man in Northern Cyprus might have come across something about six months ago. We think he has a girl who visits him in Cyprus from time to time. She is being monitored as we speak.'

Nasir Al-din looked angry, he said 'You think? Think? Why don't you know? Six months of surveillance, three months of which have been intense, of the girl and not a whisper of a connection to Xanthis. Why is it taking so long to get results?'

'Sir, at first I was not sure if the information was right. This girl is not like the others. She does not fit into the normal pattern of Xanthis' women. Ever since your instructions to keep an eye on Xanthis two years ago, we have been doing just that. The women he has are of a certain type. They are usually in their thirties and are provided with all manner of luxuries. For example, Xanthis had this French girl. It was very discreet. She visited Cyprus for two weeks twice a year. That was a year ago. She stayed in the same local hotel and he was a frequent visitor to the hotel. The chambermaids confirm that he was seen ascending the lift and getting out at the floor that she had her room.

He was also spotted with her in Paris. She, unlike the English girl lives very comfortably. Nice apartment, flashy car, doesn't work, spends plenty of money on shopping. Also, we found out that she recently had cosmetic surgery. Expensive surgery for a woman without visible means of support. Paid for by Xanthis we presume. We thought she would provide us with something useful but apart from her telling a girlfriend, our source, that they once broke the hotel bed while screwing, she really could not or would not say anything else. Doesn't want to lose her goose that lays the golden eggs. In any case, we believe that ever since Cathy Burkert came on the scene, she is out of favour.'

'Our suspicions about Miss Burkert were alerted not because of any of the usual reasons. Unlike the others, Miss Burkert is in her twenties and lives very modestly. She works very hard for a living, shares a flat with a girlfriend, has an old car, and does not have expensive clothes or jewellery – we checked. She only came to our attention because she has been in the same place and at the same time as Xanthis on three different occasions. All official functions with official photographs. And there she is in the background. One of Xanthis men who talked said he knew her to be there in an official capacity as an interpreter but it doesn't make sense her being flown out from London on a couple of occasions to Cyprus, when he can get hold of so many interpreters locally. That is why Sir I decided to have her watched. And it has paid off – in a very, very different way.' Igor smiled chillingly.

'Go on' barked Al-din

'Sir we believe just today, we have stumbled across something of great value to us. We believe we can get to Xanthis now. You see, Cathy Burkert is psychokinetic which means she can move or control objects using the mind. Do you remember the Israeli Uri Geller? Well, Miss Burkert does similar stuff. Far more importantly, she is also a telepathist. We monitored a conversation where she was being told of her ability. I spoke to my contact who is ex-KGB and he had some very interesting information.'

Al-din looked impatient, 'What the fuck has that to do with anything? Psycho Kinesis! Telepathy...Bah!'

The Russian said, 'Yes. Have you heard of transhumanists?'

The Russian took one look at Al-din's face and hastily added. 'There are a group of scientists and intellectuals who believe that telepathy enhanced by technology will be the inevitable future of humanity.

Dr. Kevin Warwick of the University of Reading, England is one of the leading experts holding this view, and has based all his recent Cybernetics R&D around developing practical, safe devices for directly connecting human nervous systems together with computers and with each other.

He believes techno-enabled telepathy - psycho-electronics is another term used - will become the sole or at least the primary form of human communication in the future. I spoke to my friend, Dimitri, who is ex-KGB-a disillusioned operative who worked as a double agent for the CIA, who believes that such technology is in existence. I also mentioned Miss Burkert's unusual talents and Dimitri got very excited. He alluded to experiments and findings, and the upshot of it is that I believe, it would be an easy matter to coerce Xanthis to see things our way, using Miss Burkert as a mental conduit.'

Al-din looked extremely irritated and sceptical, 'Igor don't waste my time. I don't believe that such technology has been developed'

'Indeed it has. I will explain how such technology works. There are precedents. Let me take you back to the fifties and radio-waves developed by the CIA. Dr. Warwick in England is using safe, openly transparent, methods but the CIA developed a highly-secret project where the remit was to get control of an individual to the point where he would do the CIA's bidding against his own will.

The race was on to create a programmable assassin!'

'Sir' said Igor. Igor paused to silently congratulate himself yet again on his dealings with Al-din. He made sure he was always careful to maintain a respectful note when speaking to his very rich and powerful cousin, 'A crack CIA team was formed that could travel, at a moment's notice, to anywhere in the world. Their task was to test the new interrogation techniques, and ensure that victims would not remember being interrogated and programmed. All manner of narcotics, from marijuana to LSD, heroin and sodium pentathol (the so called 'truth drug') - 'narcohypnosis' were regularly used on unwitting US citizens.'

Al-din said, 'I remember reading something about this scandal years ago'

Igor said, 'Yes, it all came to light in the seventies through revealing documents being misfiled. Although precisely how extensive illegal testing became will never be known - Following public outrage, the CIA announced it had ceased its mind manipulation programmes but this was untrue. CIA efforts increasingly focused on psycho-electronics- computers- synthetic telepathy, you know?'

Al- din said, 'Computers, machines –Synthetic telepathy? How is this done? Explain!'

Igor glowed with self-satisfaction. He had done his homework. He said pompously, 'Pulsed microwaves create an auditory sensation,' he broke off for Al-din was drumming his fingers impatiently on the desk.

'Bear with me cousin Nasr. At first they used to implant a small probe into the brain and after testing successfully they concluded that motion, emotion and behaviour can be directed by electrical forces. Humans could be controlled like robots by push buttons. Huge leaps in technology brought them to 'microwaves'. The field of Electromagnetism.'

Igor looked at the notes in his hand. He had prepared well knowing Al-din would want to be briefed thoroughly. 'Cousin, everything in life has a frequency. A radio wave, the human mind, even a brick wall. If you consider the humble mobile phone which converts speech into radio waves and then back to speech, as long as the frequency is known.

Let me tell you about a scientist, funded by the DOD, one J.F.Scapitz (this method of mind-control has become known in the trade as an 'A. Scapitz')who in 1974, combined earlier hypnosis studies with emerging microwave technology and proved that the spoken word of the hypnotist could be conveyed to the subconscious parts of the brain. He claimed this could be achieved without implanting any technical devices for 'receiving or transcoding messages'.

'Are you saying that unlike Warwick's theory you don't have to be hooked up to any machine- no connection of human nervous systems?'

'No, not at all. For the first time, US agents had the ability to remotely tamper with an individual's mind. Scapitz went even further, claiming that this could be achieved without the target even becoming aware of what was happening. Today the method exists where speech can be sent over a low-frequency signal to a human subject, where, when the subject's brainwave frequency is known, can deliver that speech pattern directly into the human's mind and would be conceived as a "thought"

This is where Cathy Burkert starts to become useful. She has the vital ingredient, higher than normal levels of psychokinetic capabilities. She is also a telepathist, naturally. People like her are born with high outputs of electrical energy. Yes, sir, nature has programmed her to be receptive. We can exploit this, cousin. You see, if we can identify Cathy Burkert's brain frequency, and with a suitable piece of electronic wizardry, she would be able to receive our instructions directly into her mind without any knowledge that we are feeding her those "ideas". On the other hand, perhaps if she was made aware..she could serve us better!

'And this is synthetic telepathy?'

'Yes, today, the ability to remotely transmit microwave voices inside a target's head is known inside the Pentagon as "Synthetic telepathy". According to a Dr. Robert Becker, *"Synthetic Telepathy has applications in covert operations designed to drive a target crazy with voices or deliver undetected instructions to a programmed assassin"*

'You are exaggerating, I am sure. Besides, I have no intention of killing Xanthis. He needs to be tortured whilst he is alive and useful. Come my Slavic relative, explain what this has to do with Xanthis? Are you proposing that we use a machine on Miss Burkert – to brainwash her- to get to Xanthis. Why not use it directly on Xanthis?

'Sir, Xanthis is too heavily protected. His surroundings are swept electronically. We would never be able to create the field we need, not continuously.

Moreover, Xanthis has no extra-sensory perception that would make his mind malleable'

Al- din's smile was twisted. He said, 'Mind control. I like it. Thank God for the age of computers. By the way, where are we to get such a machine that combines the two fields - electromagnetism and hypnosis? On the internet maybe?' He added sarcastically.

The Russian said calmly, 'As a matter of fact Sir, my source in Russia is already looking for a just such a device. But we have may struck gold already!

Igor, his thin lips contorted into a feral grin, was feeling replete with self-satisfaction. He said, 'London has confirmed that Burkert has been speaking to a healer by the name of Matthew Mallard. Mallard is famous in certain circles relating to paranormal behaviour. He also conducted experiments in the 70's relating to mind control and machines. From his conversations with Burkert, he is the man who seems to be pushing her to recognise her psychic abilities. I find that suspect. The recent conversations he has had with Burkert, also reveal his intentions of using her abilities as a conduit- in fact, that's why I got interested! I have asked my men to check him out. I am certain he has a hidden agenda. It can only help us.'

Al-din frowned fiercely, 'Listen my Russian cousin, time is of the essence.' He paused and considered. Al-din's mind quickly worked out the possibilities. 'Can the machine be traced back to us?'

'That's the beauty of it Sir, as far as the general public know, such technology does not exist' said Igor. 'In fact my friend, Dimitri, the ex- KGB man had to be bribed heavily to divulge this information. Igor coughed at Al-din's sharp look. He said hastily, 'I am sure it will be a worthwhile investment'

'Igor, I want all the angles covered. Make absolutely sure it's foolproof. Because, cousin, you lowly worm, if we were to get such a machine, Xanthis would not be the only target. My enemies would be like dust. He laughed suddenly. 'Isn't technology wonderful!' We need to take good care of Miss Burkert'. He pointed to his head. 'Up here'

'I'm already on to it' Igor said hastily.

Nasr Al-din steepled his fingers together on his desk. His tone was icy, 'Keep on it. Also check Cathy Burkert's background. Anything that we can use as leverage'

Chapter 9

Nasr Al-din drove his red Ferrari fast down the deserted road. He had just attended a high-level meeting which had extended late into the night. He looked at the clock on the dashboard- it was 3 a.m, he was tired but he needed to get to his office to sort out some papers. Nasr lit up a cigar- Cuban, the best, as he parked the car. The meeting he had just attended had been with two men, one the head of Turkish Intelligence and a government minister- both bastards, he thought privately but the information they had provided and their support was vital to him setting up operations in Cyprus.

Nasr had mulled over the information on the mind-control machine and the process used –what had Igor called it – 'Ascapitz?'. He had decided to run with it. He had advised Igor to use all efforts, no expense spared, to find such technology – with the Russian market being wide-open these days, Nasr did not doubt the acquisition of such a machine. Hence the meet with the two men earlier. He needed them to pave the way in Cyprus- North and South- to establish a base of operations.

After reassuring them repeatedly that the machine was undetectable, they had begun to realise how fortunate a position they could be in – especially when it came to getting rid of Al-din's and indeed Turkey's, arch-foe Xanthis. That fucker needed to be diverted away from the no vote and away from the Armenian -dare–he-bloody-say-it–'genocide', -watching his words, thought Al-din, was a constant exercise in the hyper-sensitive climate that existed here in Ankara.

Bismillah, these mainland Turks were so sensitive, any words or deeds which could be construed as 'insulting' Turkishness could be punished by an actual law enforced about insulting their national identity.

Al-din had been promised lucrative payment for getting rid of Xanthis.

However, as Nasr Al-din, now sitting at his desk, turned his attention to the papers in front of him, he knew that Hektor Xanthis would prove a tough nut to crack. He was no ordinary man. He could not be bribed. He had a surplus of power and money. He was the one man who had the Cypriot President's ear, the one bastard most likely to succeed, rumoured to be groomed to be the next President.

Nasr himself had tried to convince the majority of Turkey's political hierarchy of the extent of the threat that Hektor Xanthis was but they would not listen to him. Instead it had come to his attention that some ministers considered him, Nasr, an extremist. Nasr shrugged off such accusations. Now, because of

'Ascapitz', he at least had the ear of two influential men and they were making the right noises.

He had decided to mount a covert operation. Once he succeeded he knew that they would offer him a stake in the gas pipeline that was planned.

Two years ago Nasr had approached them but they had refused. Nasr had known then that Europe was looking to bolster their dwindling gas supplies. A gas pipeline was planned bringing gas from the Caspian and Middle Eastern areas via Turkey through to Europe. Nasr wanted in on it. His empire already comprised property and hotels, but he wanted more, much more. First Cyprus has to be sorted– that bastard Xanthis!

For an instant Nasr had a flashback to the old days in Northern Cyprus where he

Nasr Al-din had been born in Kyrenia to Turkish parents in the North of Cyprus in 1960. His parents owned a shop and had only the one child. He lived happily with his Greek neighbours and had one particular friend Hektor Xanthis who was the same age as him. They loved messing about in boats by the harbour and considered themselves lucky that Nasr's uncle allowed them to play on his tourist cruiser. They were golden days and Nasr, though secretly envious of Xanthis, was also extremely possessive of his friend. He would go to great lengths to convince Hektor that he Nasr should be the only one that Hektor played with. At school they sat together and during break Nasr would always steer Hektor to one side, hoping they would be left alone by the other boys.

Unfortunately for Nasr, Hektor Xanthis excelled at sport and hence was very popular and his friendship was sought after. Nasr on the other hand was the last to get involved in any strenuous physical activity. Nasr hating every minute that his friend was not at his side nevertheless resigned himself to waiting on the sidelines. Sometimes he wished secretly that Hektor would get an injury so that he could no longer be involved in sport. No matter, Nasr knew there was one area that he would not get left behind. Because academically they were in constant competition with one another, both being evenly matched.

Their differences started to show when both boys were in their teens. When they were children they were totally unaware of the undercurrents that existed between the Greeks and the Turkish races in Cyprus because in their village everybody lived happily together. The boys were fourteen when, in a sleepy village in the foothills of the Five Finger mountains not far from Kyrenia, the news drifted through, Turkey was preparing to advance. The Greek Cypriots were advised to leave and head for the south. It took two days for Nasr's whole world to be turned upside down.

Hektor Xanthis and his family were leaving - The treachery. How could Hektor and his family desert the North? Nasr knew that they would be treated fairly by the advancing Turks but being cowards they had to run. Nasr felt a terrible pain- an immense loss for his boyhood friend- was it then that he first realised his sexual inclination? Nasr, a big personality trapped in a stocky frame, felt an instant self-loathing at his attraction to Xanthis. At that moment flames of hatred started burning in Nasr's mind. He decided he hated Hektor for being Greek. He hated him because he was leaving and leaving Nasr alone and friendless behind. Desperately he thought that maybe there was a way that Hektor could be forced to remain. Hektor had sworn him to secrecy saying that his father trusted the Al-din's with the information of the Xanthis' family's imminent departure.

Nasr decided that he owed Hektor no loyalty. He had been told the Turks were advancing swiftly from the port of Famagusta, their entry point into Northern Cyprus. He decided they must be informed. Surely they would stop the Xanthis family from leaving. Nasr ran all the way to his uncle's house. His uncle was an important man. He would know what to do.

Nasr's mouth twisted with bitterness as he remembered the rest. How his uncle had informed the Turkish major and they had rushed to the Xanthis house only to find it empty with the family already departed in the early hours of that morning. The Turkish major had ridiculed his uncle. His uncle in turn had taken it out on Nasr and harangued him to such an extent that Nasr had lost it. Nasr had hit his uncle. Nasr was a strapping fourteen year old and his uncle a small man, and the punch had knocked his uncle to the ground. Nasr looked on in a daze as his uncle's head smashed on the pavement. Bystanders saw the boy Nasr stand and stare at the fallen body. They rushed Nasr's uncle to the hospital.

Nasr's uncle never regained consciousness. For the next four years until his death, he remained in a coma and Nasr grew to be an adult with the constant reminder of his actions. He was considered the pariah of the village. He had no friends. The boys would jeer at him and the girls would look at him only to make fun of him.

Nasr bided his time. One day he would leave. He had plans to go to mainland Turkey and make his fortune. And then he was going hunting. Nasr had had four long years for his hatred to consolidate into an acrid core of steel- he knew who was really to blame for his misfortunes. In Nasr's young mind he attached all blame to Xanthis. For Nasr reasoned that the entire chain of events hinged on the lie Xanthis had told him.

Xanthis had said that the family would be leaving that night but instead they had left in the morning. The catastrophe that had befallen Nasr as a result, was because of Hektor Xanthis' lie. A simple matter of timing and the Xanthis family would even now be incarcerated in a Turkish jail, perhaps even missing like so many other Greek families. The hate based on a simple lie corroded Nasr, twisted him inside out when he thought of his isolation from the rest of his community. Hektor Xanthis would pay. One day Nasr would be in a position to hurt him. Death was too easy for Xanthis. The only just punishment was to make his life a living hell.

Which brought him back to the present.

Nasr carried on attending to business matters, he checked his watch later, it was well into the afternoon, he decided to call Abdullah. Wake the big bastard up. What the fuck do I pay him huge sums of money for?

Nasr was almost disappointed when Abdullah's voice answered bright and chirpy although the voice became nervous when he realised it was the great man Nasr on the other end. Nasr had forgotten that it was mid-day in the UK. He listened as Abdullah filled him in on the details.

'I want results and I want them quick. No excuses. Acele etmek, cabuk olmak, (come on, get a move on), Abdel'

Chapter 10

The room was dusty and full of books and there were rolls of parchment on a desk in the corner. Cathy, Malcolm and Tessa stood in front of the desk where a small man hurriedly summoned an assistant to bring chairs. 'Don't worry he said. You will not be working in this room.' He shook their hands. 'My name is Dr. Andreas Michaelides. I will take you to the room where the best of our Greek scholars have been examining the papyri. As you know we have had to have verification from a number of other experts before we can go public with this. That is why we have asked you here to translate and therefore authenticate the documents.

'I presume all the necessary carbon-dating has been carried out' said Malcolm

'Yes, The Laboratory of Archaeometry in Greece dates it to 6th century BC which is precisely around the time the Cypria was written. Are you familiar with the Cypria? asked Michaelides

Tessa said, 'My understanding of the *Cypria* is sketchy. I believe there is some doubt who actually wrote it. Was it Homer?'

'Let me explain, said Michaelides with a smile at Cathy. Cathy smiled back. He obviously loves telling the story, she thought. Cathy in fact had done some research into the subject but was too shy to steal this affable man's thunder.

Michaelides said, 'STASINUS, of Cyprus, according to some ancient authorities is the author of the *Cypria*, which is one of the poems belonging to the epic cycle. Others ascribed it to Hegesias of Salamis or even to Homer himself, who was said to have written it on the occasion of his daughter's marriage to Stasinus.

The *Cypria,* presupposed an acquaintance with the events of the Homeric Iliad and thus formed a kind of introduction to the *Iliad.* Whilst Homer's Iliad was a detailed account of the war fought at Troy between the Achaeans and the Trojans, *the Cypria* deals with the events that led up to the cause of the war and the journey of the Achaeans to begin that ten-year battle. It contained an account of the judgment of Paris, the rape of Helen, the abandonment of Philoctetes on the island of Lemnos, the landing of the Achaeans on the coast of Asia, and the first engagement before Troy.

Michaelides continued, "That brings us to why you are here. We need to establish definitively whether it is Homer's work. With your combined knowledge of ancient Greek and your expertise, Malcolm as a philologist, whereby the grammar, rhetoric, history and interpretation of the papyri will confirm its authorship…Ah but I am stating what is obvious to you three. Forgive me, I am very excited about this.

Malcolm said, 'What has led you to believe that it is not one of the other authors you mentioned earlier, Stasinas or Hegesias? What precisely made you rule the others out? Why definitely Homer?'

Dr Michaelides beamed, 'I have been saving that information till the last. We believe we have uncovered in some of the papyri the writings of two men. As you are aware before the Iliad and the Odyssey were written down, Homer was a travelling bard who recited to his audience tales of his epics.' Michaelides jumped out of his chair. He could not get the words out fast enough in his excitement. 'Well, you can imagine our good fortune- this is the first time that the world has heard of men who actually attended Homer's recital and who have written of their experience! These two men refer to extracts from the

Iliad, the Odyssey and yes I can see from your faces the *Cypria*. We believe this information and the other pages of papyri which refers to Philoctetes on Lemnos will definitively prove that Homer was the author of all three epics - For centuries there has been a question mark hanging over whether Homer was actually the author of the *Iliad* and the *Odyssey* and the *Cypria*. But Now the papyri has been found – but no my friends, I do not want my opinion and the research my team and I have carried out to influence you in any way. Your combined expert opinion has to be arrived at independently. But have your Cyprus coffee and I will introduce you to the other members of my department and show you where you will be working.'

That evening Cathy sipped her glass of white wine on the hotel balcony and breathed in the scent of jasmine. The evening air was balmy. Cathy loved Cyprus. She had visited it three times before. Cathy smiled and thought – ostensibly for business but the pleasure had been breathtaking. This was Cathy's first time in Cyprus' capital city Nicosia. A divided city with the Ledra gates separating the Turkish North from the Greek South. Cathy thought of her first visit to Cyprus and so far her favourite place in Cyprus. Paphos in the south-west corner of Cyprus. Hektor had arranged the visit as he had arranged the subsequent two. Officially she had been hired as an interpreter of Ancient Greek but she had barely done any translating. Instead she had spent stolen hours with Hektor in Paphos. 'Let's hope I get a couple of days off to visit Paphos this time', thought Cathy

Cathy was tired but excited about the papyri. She decided to order room service for dinner. She didn't feel up to going downstairs to the restaurant. It had been a long day of discussion, planning and in Cathy's case, instruction. They had decided to divide the twenty-six pages between them. Andreas Michaelides had explained that just ten pages were to do with Philoctetes at Lemnos. The pages were obviously a fragment of an account of the time that Philoctetes lived in Lemnos. Why did Philo (Cathy decided to abbreviate his name for her own use) leave the rest of the Achaean force who were headed for Troy? Cathy's knowledge of the details was limited. 'I must ask Malcolm', she thought. Malcolm had taken charge of those precious pages on Phil at Lemnos. They had made copies of the originals, by hand. Cathy's section contained eight pages. This was the account of one of the men, Morpheus, who had attended Homer's recital. Tessa had the remaining section, the Leander pages. Cathy had no idea how to conduct exploratory analysis on such a document. Malcolm had given her a crash course on it this afternoon. Cathy had made notes. She consulted them now. 'What had Malcolm said?'

'That's it. The American scholar Millman Parry published findings that showed that oral poetry, performed by bards such as Homer, is performed in front of an illiterate audience by an equally illiterate poet, who he maintained, improvises his poem as it progresses.'

'What were the clues though she was looking for? Her notes said repeated lines, phrases –oh I'd better clarify some of these points' Cathy decided to speak to Malcolm. She dialled reception who put her through.

Cathy said, 'Malcolm hope I'm not disturbing. She listened to his 'no, of course not my dear'

Cathy said 'Just remembered something that you said about formulae in the text. I wasn't completely clear to the finer points. I'm sorry to seem so ignorant. I realise I am no substitute for a researcher'

'My dear, it's great that you were included on this trip because an untutored mind like yours might have a whole different slant. Do not feel inadequate, Yes, I mentioned Millman Parry earlier. He was a great chap. Made a study of traditional oral poetry which was being sung by illiterate Serbo-Croatian singers and came up with some explanations. Homer's poems contain many recurring themes and typical scenes such as the sending of a message, the arrival of a messenger, or of a stranger or guest, the offering of hospitality, with meals and baths, the homecoming of someone who has been absent for a long time, etc. When Homer wished to describe Dawn for example, he used identical words on every occasion. Are you with me so far, Cathy?'

'Yes. Do go on.'

'Homer as any other oral poet in composing his poem selected and combined such traditional themes, using the formulae with which they are associated in his repertoire. And by a process of analogy, he could adapt his existing stock of formulae to fit new themes or ideas, or the particular situation of his present narrative. To speak in layman's terms, basically what you are looking for in Morpheus account, are familiar Homeric themes and phrases. Cathy, I suggest you make a list of them and I will look over them in the morning.'

Cathy said, Thanks Malcolm. I'll get onto that straightaway. Goodnight. See you in the morning.' Cathy put the phone down.

The next instant her mobile rang. Her mother's voice said anxiously, 'Cathy your eldest brother has been in contact.' Cathy started in shock. 'Mark? But we have not heard from him in years. I thought he was in Australia.'

'Apparently he was out there until recently. Cathy', her mother said, 'I'm worried. He was asking the strangest questions. Mostly about you. Funny but he seemed to know the answers already. Have you been keeping in touch with him?'

'Mum, Cathy said, you know that Mark and I have never got along. I haven't seen him or spoken to him for years. And I can't imagine from where he would have any information about me. We have no mutual acquaintance'

'Anyway, her Mother said, I was pleased to hear from him. He has promised to come and see me. I expect you are having a nice time in Cyprus?

Five minutes later Cathy switched the phone off. 'So, she thought the bad penny turns up again. God when was the last time I saw Mark? It must have been at Dad's funeral. Six years ago. Cathy remembered that year only too well. She felt bitterness wash over her.

Once the memory was resurrected, it invaded Cathy's mind. God, she had been so young.

Cathy was eighteen and a rare beauty. She had inherited her mother's olive skin and black hair but it was from her father that she had got the big green eyes. She was 5ft 8, had a figure like a dream and all the boys in the street were in love with her. The boys sensed and the men saw the raw sexuality in the full red lips, the waist-length black hair and the way she moved. But Cathy was totally unconscious of all the attention she aroused. He head was mostly buried in books. She would read at night when all the rest were asleep. She had to steal out into the hallway by the front door where there was a lamp, so as not to disturb her sister Fiona with whom she shared a room. Even though Fiona slept so soundly that nothing disturbed her. Cathy wished with all her heart that Fiona was a light sleeper. It would have saved Cathy so much anguish five years ago. But Mark didn't touch her any more, not since she had threatened him with a knife. Thank God that was sorted now. Although she still didn't feel safe at night. However, she liked being in the armchair near the front door. Easy to escape. She would curl up in the chair, cold but strangely warmed by the words she read. School was finally over and she had done well. 'I've done well enough to go to University and that's where I'm setting my sights. I've got to get away from the grinding poverty and from that bastard Mark. Let's hope I get the job tomorrow' That night Cathy went to bed early. She knew she had to look her best the next day.

Early the next morning, as she waited for the bus that was to take her to the train station, Cathy reflected bitterly how little her life had changed since her father's illness had confined him to hospital nearly six months ago. She, her sister and younger brother

Harry, had exchanged one tyrant for another with Mark the oldest brother dominating and bullying them. He was known to take the occasional swipe at Harry although he didn't dare touch the girls with Mum around. But Cathy knew that he had a vile temper and his rages could be uncontrollable.

But his verbal abuse ran unabated. He would shout at them and threaten them continually. Life was such shit, thought Cathy. No, I will not be despondent, she said to herself, the next instant. I am going to University. I just need to earn some money first. Today is hopefully going to be the first step to achieving my goals.

Cathy loved London. The cosmopolitan atmosphere, the lovely old buildings, the names of streets so familiar from Monopoly. One day she thought I shall live here. Oh I do hope I look good. Cathy knew the modelling agency had advertised for girls taller than she was but she was going to go along and try anyway.

Jeremy Watson looked up from the Hasselblad camera and feasted his eyes on her face. She was gorgeous, a natural. He'd shot her in different poses, adjusting the lighting and backdrops. Great body too. He said, 'let's see how these come out. Are you able to hang around for a couple of hours?' Cathy nodded.

'Great', he smiled at her, 'don't look so scared. You did great for your first time'

Two hours later Cathy viewed the photos. 'Hmm, she thought, I wonder if everyone has a problem looking at themselves objectively.' The boys at school had said she was a babe and were constantly trying to chat her up but Cathy took no notice of them. She preferred her own company. Sometimes during break she would hang around with the other girls. With very little effort Cathy was a popular member of the class.

She was funny and chatty when she was in a group and no-one ever guessed the miserable life she endured at home. Cathy would never invite anyone to her home. Cathy preferred to have a host of acquaintances rather than close friends. There was no chance of exchanging confidences that way.

It would be nice though to have a confidante, thought Cathy as she took the train home that evening. She sighed and crossed her fingers as she thought of Jeremy's parting words. I'm going to submit these photos to the client first thing tomorrow, he had said. You have a good chance of getting the contract. Seeing her anxious look he'd winked at her and added, 'a very good chance'

Cathy was keeping her fingers crossed. Cathy settled herself into the sofa that evening. Fiona was out visiting a friend but Harry was home and Mum in her *favourite chair with her sewing on her lap. Their peace was soon to be shattered.*

Mark Burkert was drunk. He had spent the entire evening at the pub with his loutish mates. He opened the front door and entered the tiny living room. 'Shit, he said Fucking hell. I'm out of fags again.' Seeing Cathy, Harry and his mother turn their eyes away from the television and towards him, he sneered and said to Harry, 'Go and get me some fags from the corner shop, you little shit.' Cathy's mother said, 'Stop using such language. You are late. Have you been doing overtime?' 'You wish mamma mia, you wish!'

'Mark you are drunk, said Cathy 'Harry if Mark wants cigarettes I'm sure he can get them himself'

Mark said, 'Listen you bitch, have you found a job yet? No use looking to me for hand-outs. I'm not working all day at that lousy salesman's job so you can benefit. Mamma don't you give her anything' He turned to Cathy, ' Whatever you get in your miserable life, miss high and mighty, you will have to earn it' He aimed his foot at Harry and kicked him viciously in the knee, 'What did I just say? Are you Deaf, dumb and stupid, as the old man would say. Speaking of that rotting carcass -How is my father?' His words were slurred. Lucia looked shocked.

She said 'Mark he is getting worse. You know he doesn't recognise me anymore.' 'Well old lady that's what Alzheimer's does to you. Harry your time is up. GO!' Cathy looked at Harry's face. He was trying not to show fear. He was almost a man at fifteen and he hated being belittled and bullied by his brother. He sat in the chair said with a set mouth. 'I'm not going'

The next instant Mark who was teetering had hauled him to his feet and was about to bring his open hand to the side of Harry's face when Cathy from behind pushed Mark. Mark turned and the blow that *was meant for Harry smashed into the side of Cathy's jaw. She cried out in pain and then felt another hard slap to the other side of her face, then another and another.*

For what seemed like hours Mark's hand kept on smashing into either side of her face. Her mother's voice screaming, 'Stop it Mark. Please stop.' finally got through the haze in Mark's head; he looked at Cathy who had collapsed onto the sofa and was curled up with her hands to her face. 'You have been asking for that for a long time, you fucked-up bitch'. The next thing they heard the front-door slamming. Harry and her mother looked in shock at Cathy's swollen face. It was blue and purple with bruises already forming.

'Harry get some frozen peas, ice, quickly from the freezer.' 'My goodness Cathy you must not interfere with Mark. You know Mark has a vicious temper. Just like his father.

Lucia was crying. She took Cathy's hand 'I am sorry I cannot control him. He must leave the house. He must live elsewhere. I will speak to the priest tomorrow. He will help us.' Cathy held the bag of peas to her face, the icy cold soothing the raw flesh. Lucia said, *'I want you and Harry to say nothing and when your sister gets home I will tell her too. We cannot tell anybody that Mark hit you. We never told anybody about your father's beatings. Now we mustn't tell anybody of Mark. For my sake. I couldn't live with the shame. Not after all I went through with your father and the shame when the callers would shout for the return of their money. No I cannot live with any more shame. We will say nothing'*

'Oh mum', groaned Cathy looking at the face in the hallway mirror. 'I'm waiting to hear from a modelling agency tomorrow. Look at my face!' Tears slipped down her cheeks involuntarily. 'I will never get the job *looking like this. Any other job at my age will not give me enough money to cover three years of University.'* Lucia said nothing. She wrung her hands and cried softly. Cathy went to her bedroom and sat on the bed filled with despair. But Cathy got lucky.

The client, a cosmetics giant not only gave her a lucrative contract, they also agreed to wait six weeks until she could start sitting for a photo-shoot. Cathy could now afford to rent her own place. She moved to a shared flat close to central London. Her father died six months later and at the funeral, Cathy did not cry. She felt frozen. She stared at Mark icily and said not a word to him.

A year later Cathy quit her lucrative modelling contract and went to University. She had made good her promise. Things were looking up. Cathy loved Uni, she was doing well, she had met Jeremy who looked out for her. But tragedy was to strike, at a time when Cathy *was confident and felt cherished and loved for the first time in her life. Cathy did not cry at Jeremy's funeral. She was a survivor.*

Chapter 11

The sound of her phone ringing brought Cathy out of the memories of those dark days. Feeling disorientated by the remembrance of violence unleashed Cathy said 'hello' into the phone hesitantly. Her mother's words of Mark asking questions about her came to mind and she almost expected to hear his dreaded voice hounding her. But the next instant Cathy melted at the sound of the callers accented tones.

'I got your message. So you are here. How long will you be staying for?' said Hektor. He added 'I have missed you'- the words were music to Cathy's ears.

She said, 'Can we meet?'

'Actually I am very busy at the moment. But I will try and manage an hour or two. Call me tomorrow. I will come to Nicosia. Have a good night'

Cathy put the phone down, all the darkness of earlier memories dispelled. She felt as though she was floating on air.

'My god and to think I did not want anything to do with him at first. How can such happiness be wrong?' she said aloud.

Cathy thought back to the beginning of their relationship and how she had resisted his continued phone calls. Until she had bumped into him at an embassy do. Cathy had taken one look at him and known the inevitable. God they hadn't stayed long at the embassy.

Cathy had been tongue-tied. It had been difficult to breathe as they gazed at each other. He too had been strangely affected and he had suggested they go to his hotel. The door had barely closed to his hotel suite when they were in each other's arms. Cathy remembered fingers in secret places, tongues probing passionately, her delicate wisps of lace on the floor before her breasts were suckled.

Then he muttered, 'I have to have you. Yes? Do you agree? His tongue was in her ear. Cathy, her eyes dark with passion, whispered 'yes oh yes'

He was inside her and Cathy knew that no matter what happened in her life, she would not be able to do without this man. She was tied to him by this act - This fusion of their bodies.

Thinking about it was turning Cathy on. She hastily set about getting her papers together before she started preparing for bed. She thought back to what he had said about being busy. She wondered if it was anything to do with the referendum on Cyprus. She knew that was due to be held soon and the newspapers which she had briefly scanned were full of it. The Greek Cypriots did not like the Kofi Annan plan. It gave too much to the Northern element. Cathy had been surprised to see

Hektor's picture in the papers. The story underneath had suggested that he might be a president-in-waiting. Cathy wondered how the papers had got hold of it. When she had met him six months ago in Paphos, Hektor had mentioned it softly to her and had also said to keep it confidential. As if Cathy thought, she would ever tell. Apart from her flatmate, Alison, no one knew about Hektor. Her mother only knew that she had a friend in Cyprus, even the sex of the friend had never been mentioned by Cathy.

'No wonder, thought Cathy, he takes such precautions! Any hint of a scandal and he would be destroyed. Cathy realised now why these days he would never make contact initially. She always phoned him and would leave a message with his minders and he would call her back. They would speak quickly and arrange to meet. Cathy presumed that was what would happen tomorrow.

The next day she went through the same routine of calling him and leaving a message with his minder. It was mid-morning and she was sitting at a desk with the translation before her. Things were speeding up with Malcolm sitting across from her, beaming as he sat engrossed with the work. This was their third day and the work was going well. Cathy hoped that Malcolm would give Tessa and herself some clue as to the story of Philoctetes on Lemnos but so far he was keeping things very close to his chest. Cathy picked up her translation, the account of Morpheus, one of the witnesses to Homer's recitals. Supposedly Homer, she added to herself. She pored over it. The translation itself had been easy. Extracts from the *Iliad* and the *Odyssey,* she had cross-referenced and the stories were fairly accurate. However the words that Homer was purported to have used in the witness' account did not exactly match the original.

Cathy's mobile rang. It was Hektor. Cathy quickly left her desk and walked into the empty corridor. Hektor gave her the name of the hotel and the time. She said she would be there and he rang off. Cathy took the phone away from her ear and started worrying that he had sounded tense. She began to feel anxious and wondered if he was getting tired of her. After all she was not the only woman he saw. Cathy thought, 'I may be young but I'm not stupid. I see him on an average once in 4 months and I know with his sex-drive he must need women on a regular basis.'

For the millionth time Cathy wondered what she saw in him. He was twenty years her senior, fairly tall, an ascetic looking man. His attraction surely had to do with his power. She was perfectly aware that with her background, his immense wealth represented a wall of security. Financial security that she never had as a child.

But funnily enough she would never accept anything from him. Once at the beginning, he tried to give her jewellery. She threw a tantrum and told him where he could stuff it. He had also offered her financial help if she needed it. She had firmly refused. He never tried to give her anything again.

Hektor was a highly sexual man. Was that it? Cathy knew just the thought of his actions when they had sex was enough to get her into an aroused state. Their affair had been going on now for about a year and a half and Cathy still felt besotted with him. To Cathy he was her primordial mate. Her passion for him was all-consuming.

They would meet usually in a five star hotel. Cathy would take a seat in the lobby and await his call to tell her the room number.

He would arrange the room. She never knew how he did it. She guessed it had something to do with his minders working out the minor details, like booking the room, leaving the room door ajar so all she had to do was step into the room and shut the door after her. He would join her a few minutes later. She had the suspicion that he was in another room a few doors away and once he was convinced she wasn't being followed, he would enter the room.

'Can't wait to see him', thought Cathy now. She began to feel shivery in anticipation of their date.

Cathy managed to get away after having a quick lunch with Malcolm and Tessa. She took a taxi to the hotel. She was on time and trying to quell the butterflies in her tummy.

Just a couple of minutes and I will be in his arms, thought Cathy. Cathy took her seat.

Ten minutes later, Cathy thought, today is different. Firstly he was late. That meant exposure for Cathy. She was sitting in the hotel reception waiting. She knew hers was a face that was not easily forgettable. She glanced at the man seated across from her. He was swarthy and she was sure she had seen him before. Was he one of Hektor's men? Where had she seen that face? The man looked at her and looked away. He made a phone call on his mobile. A couple of minutes passed. Cathy felt uncomfortable. The receptionist was starting to take notice of Cathy. Cathy looked at her phone. Still no call. Ten minutes later and Cathy was starting to feel like a paid harlot. She had read and watched films where expensive prostitutes did the rounds of top hotels looking for customers. Cathy squirmed in her seat, wishing she could fade into the floral upholstery. Her phone rang. Hektor finally - his accented tones told her the room number.

Cathy went to the lift aware that eyes followed her movements. As she passed the swarthy man, he tried to make eye contact with her. Cathy looked straight past him. She wondered again if he was one of Hektor's men? Cathy had a feeling she had seen this man in England not in Cyprus. If he was one of Hektor's men, no doubt he regarded her as just another floozie.

Cathy sighed. 'Do I care,' she wondered. She loved Hektor and as she ascended in the lift she thought. 'It had been too long.' She hadn't seen him for six months.

Cathy thought back to the times she had been lonely longing for companionship. She had lived the life of a nun. Not that she had mentioned any of this to Hektor. Never said that she would stay in and not respond to any of the numerous invitations she received from men. She wondered if he would believe her. Even if he did, he wasn't about to change the status quo. He had his shipping empire which absorbed most of his time. He had his wife, his son plus a few women dotted around the world to assuage his sexual appetite.

Cathy thanked her lucky stars for the healer. He was her companion, her alter-ego. Someone who shared all her intimate secrets although she hadn't had the nerve to tell him about Hektor. Matt, in his turn was Cathy's secret – no one knew about him. Matt had given her so much confidence with the knowledge that she shared a special bond with him. He had said that they were the only two to be connected with each other thus - through their psychokinetic and telepathic abilities. If Matt knew about Hektor, Cathy was scared he would vilify her for it. She knew it was morally wrong to see a married man but she couldn't seem to help herself.

God, I'm pathetic, she thought. I have never thought of myself as a weak woman but Hektor has such a hold on me. It's almost primeval, this addiction to Hektor. I find myself on my way to share love and body-bonding with a man with whom there is no hope of a future, no hope of even being the only extra-marital one in his life. What is wrong with me?

Cathy forgot her misgivings the second she saw him. Hektor greeted her and kissed her after making sure the door was securely locked. Cathy had heard the rumour that his wife had caught him *in flagrante delicto* with another woman and ever since, he had been careful to lock the door. Divorce was unthinkable in Hektor's mind. His wife, a large plain jolly woman had helped him when he was struggling in getting his empire founded and he was utterly loyal to her. He never spoke of her to Cathy. He had one son, a student in Athens and he was being trained to run the father's shipping empire.

Hektor said 'We don't have much time. I have to go. I'm due at a conference in an hour'

They made love quickly passionately. Cathy felt sensation after sensation, just pure physical pleasure.

Cathy always thought of it as lovemaking by which she felt complete, a whole human being. She sighed gently as she gazed at him. They talked softly.

Hektor said, 'You know, I have told you this before- I am the leader of one of the major political parties here in Cyprus and they have asked me to consider running for president. I am seriously considering it.'

Cathy answered 'Is this something that you want to do?'

'I feel that I would like to steer the country away from the disaster that is the current Annan plan of uniting with Northern Cyprus. It is not in the Greek Cypriots favour. It does not provide adequate reparation for the land that we lost in the North, when the Turks invaded. There are other issues too.' He stroked her arm. 'But I do not want to talk politics with you. You help me relax. You are very important to me in my busy life. You have such a way of calming me'

They kissed passionately. He left shortly afterward with no mention of meeting again. Cathy had learnt to treat every encounter as it were the last.

Hektor in the 18 months she had known him had never arranged a meeting in advance. He would give her at the most twelve hours notice and she would have to drop everything to be with him. In any other man she would have never thought that she could tolerate such behaviour, such arrogance but she knew that he was unable to arrange anything due to business commitments and besides she wanted to be with him, to experience the sweetness that she believed was essentially him. Her best friend, Ally said that she was a muppet.

She would say to Cathy. 'Stop seeing him. It will destroy you in the long run. There is no future in it.'

Cathy knew that she was right. Right now, having just left Hektor and with the taste, smell and feel of him still lingering on her senses she felt such an incredible sense of happiness but Cathy knew this sort of relationship was self-destructive. I'll gather up the courage to do something about it when I return to England, she thought resolutely.

Cathy walked quickly back to her hotel. She felt a weird sensation in her head. As though she could hear voices- very faint but definitely there. The weirdest thing was that she could not hear them with her ears. She put her hands over her ears. The voices did not cease. Yes they were definitely in her mind. She strained to understand – just odd words sounding. Cathy felt scared. The next instant they stopped and she was left wondering if she had imagined it.

Chapter 12

Cathy adjusted the lamp on the desk and looked closely at the book. I must call it a night, she thought. She had been poring over the books for the last couple of hours. Was Homer ever in Cyprus? As a travelling bard he visited most of the islands but did he ever visit Cyprus? If he was in Cyprus it would add weight to the authentication of the document. She had suggested the idea to the professor and he had been enthusiastic. It was like looking for the proverbial needle. Her research so far suggested that no-one knew precisely where Homer had lived.

He had written knowledgably in the Odyssey and the Iliad of Troy and Greece and several Greek Islands but that information could have been obtained from returning Ionian sailors in the seventh century BC. Therefore to try and find out if he could feasibly have been in Cyprus was a mammoth task. She had consulted writings by other historians to see if there was a mention. She had also scheduled an early appointment the following morning with a local historian in the Department of Antiquities.

Putting the book aside, she decided to have a shower. . She hadn't had a chance to before - a quick wash had had to suffice, as straight after her meeting with Hektor the professor had rung to have a consult of their progress to date. They had met for dinner and Cathy had enjoyed her dish of Sheftalia – a local dish of pork sausages in pitta bread typical only of Cyprus, accompanied by a delicious Greek salad all washed down with a couple of glasses of the local white wine.

The professor his eyes sharply blue had looked at Cathy, 'You are looking particularly delightful. Inner glow and all that. Did you manage to get a couple of hours of sunbathing today? We noticed you had left the department early.'

Cathy went a bit red but said smoothly, 'A bit of sun, certainly but I've brought some books back to the hotel so have been doing some work in my room.'

'Well you are allowed a couple of hours off so don't look so guilty, my dear. But be careful about doing research in your room. It can get obsessive. Rather difficult to leave alone'

How right he was, thought Cathy. But it had helped to take her mind off Hektor. Always, after every sexual encounter with him, when her body was worshipped and fine-tuned with his exquisite knowledge, she sizzled with electricity and such an incredible feeling of euphoria. It was difficult to think of anything and anyone else.

Cathy let the water cascade over her in the shower and thought again of the strangeness today...such an oddity. She had been keeping it at bay just now, whilst concentrating on her work. Something had happened today, it had jolted Cathy out of her dreamy state. Firstly she had thought she was hearing voices in her head- how crazy is that? They'll have me committed if I mention it to anyone.

She had dismissed it as an aftereffect of the excitement of being with Hektor, of being in an emotionally charged state.

"Mind you, being in an emotionally charged state, Cathy Burkert,' she said aloud, 'has repercussions for you- door handles bending, metal twisting- even her postbox had been mangled...'

Cathy, in recent weeks, had been so concerned at the effects of her personal anxiety, that she thought that she needed some form of medication to calm her down. She had tried to see a doctor about it a couple of weeks ago but the waiting had been too long in the surgery and she had to reschedule. She recalled now her impatience at the wait at the surgery, she hadn't wanted to be late for an appointment at the University - the appointment that got her this job here in Cyprus.

How fortunate am I, thought Cathy, to get this job. But I must make sense of what happened today. What is the explanation for the two very disquieting things that happened - first the voices and then, my God .....calm down, take a minute to think..

Cathy stepped out of the shower and began to towel herself. Her stomach clenched as she felt a sense of panic. Was she imagining that she had been followed? It had started when she was on her way to meet Hektor, she had turned to look at one of the shop windows and had stared straight into a face, a man's in the reflection. He had looked familiar as though she had seen him before. She was sure it had been in London when she was waiting for her appointment at the doctor's. Her curiosity irked, she looked for his reflection again but he had gone. Next she thought she had recognised another man in the hotel whilst she was waiting for Hektor- one of Hektor's minders making sure that Hektor was not followed before his meeting with Cathy? Possible, but I know most of them already. But, I have definitely seen the man in the lobby before'

However, the individual incidents would not have impinged had it not seemed like a chain of unusual occurrences for on re-entering the hotel amid the plush decor of orange and brown upholstered wrought-iron chairs, looking through to the swimming pool, she had for one shocking moment believed she had seen the familiar back of the healers head.

Matthew Mallard! Cathy had said to herself, I must be mistaken. He's in London.

Surely he would have got in touch if he was here. She had been so sure it was the healer she had instinctively rushed forward to tap him on the shoulder but the man had turned the corner and by the time she got there he had disappeared.

Now considering it, Cathy felt unsettled. She suddenly remembered something weird. What had the healer said the night before she left London? Something about a machine. She had been so tired that night, she could barely recall the conversation but she was sure there had been mention of a machine and telepathy. Something was teasing at her brain. Something the healer had said. No, it's gone. Can't remember.

Cathy got into bed. She must call her flatmate Alison in the morning. Cathy had promised she would let her know how she was getting on. Alison was anxious about Cathy and her liaison with Hektor. Hang on though ,Cathy thought, Its two hours ahead here. I could call Alison now. Its only 9 pm in England. Cathy dialled the number.

Alison's voice sounded far away, muffled. 'Are you alright Ally, asked Cathy.

'I was just thinking of you, Cath, how's it going? Have you seen granddad?'

Cathy giggled even though deep down she felt irked. 'Ally, I've told you he's the most personable man...'

'Yeah, Yeah you told me. Still don't believe a girl with your beauty and your brains could find an old, greasy, married Greek attractive'
He's not at all greasy. And I love the Greek race. I love their language, that's why I studied it. I love their culture, their food and I love Cyprus.
'Then find a single Greek nearer your own age. I'm sure you have met loads of them, all dying to get close to that sexy bod of yours'.
'Yes I have met guys who find me attractive and sometimes I wish I could reciprocate but Ally, my heart is taken by Hektor Xanthis. I don't feel the remotest interest in any of the so-called eligible, available ones'
'Alright darling Cath don't wax lyrical on me pet, your life and your bed. How's the work, is it as challenging as you hoped?
'Yes, it's good. Pretty good, she repeated distractedly.

Cathy hesitated for a moment, then blurted, 'Ally, I have to tell someone, I think I'm a telepathist, as in thought transference, you know what I mean, don't you?'

'Huh? said Alison'

'Don't laugh at me please Ally, but I had the strangest thoughts today. Like someone was talking to me in my mind. I don't think I was imagining it.

'Is this before or after you saw the lover?' '

'After,' said Cathy. 'It was very odd and quite scary.'

'Hey, Cathy Burkert is this a variation of the same theme? The stuff you mentioned that you experienced with the greasy granddad. All those shivery sensations. I've never heard of anything like it'

When Cathy had first had sex with Hektor, she had been bewildered by the torrent of sensation that engulfed her when she was with him. The strange thing was sometimes she experienced the same sensations when she just thought of him. That's what had concerned her and had prompted her, albeit with great hesitation to seek Alison's advice.

Alison had at first put it down to being emotionally supercharged but could not find an explanation for Cathy shivering to such an extent as if she was in a fever. Now Alison said, 'You know Cath it's general knowledge that the brain must trigger responses to memories of intense pleasure, sadness, etc. That is why at the mere thought of Hektor your body reacts to the memory of the sensations when you were getting your leg over. No physical presence required. Although I've yet to figure out why the sensations are so exaggerated in you. Perhaps it's because you were repressed. Maybe it's something that happened in your childhood, some kind of trauma, perhaps?'

Cathy interrupted her, 'What did you just say? No physical presence required. I've been trying to think of those exact words. Ally, I've got to go. Take care I'll call again. Don't worry about me. I'll be fine.'

Cathy switched her mobile off and stared at the wall. The healer had said something about a machine and working on communicating words mentally, no physical presence required. He had used the same words.

My God, I'm going crazy, my mind is working overtime, thought Cathy. I must get to bed. It's been a long emotional day what with seeing Hektor again and all that passion. My mind is playing tricks on me. I cannot possibly give credibility to machines and mind control.

Two hours later, Cathy opened her eyes. I must be still in a dream, she thought. I can hear voices in my head. The voices are foreign. I can't understand a word. It's a language I am not familiar with. I must wake up and put a stop to this. She sat up and shook her head. I'm awake but I still hear them. Cathy put her hands to her ears to shut out the noise. The voices carried on talking - two men talking to each other - IN MY HEAD. I must not panic.

Cathy stumbled out of bed and got a glass of water. The voices went on talking. Striving to breathe normally and to stay calm, Cathy thought, I'll read something. She hurried to the desk and got her notes on Homer out. Cathy concentrated, hard. Her brows furrowed she gazed fiercely at her handwriting. The sounds in her head did not abate. A word jumped out at her, a name Malcolm. Cathy seized on the word, a real person not these disembodied voices in her head. She conjured up his face, kindly Professor Malcolm with the shock of white hair and the piercing blue eyes. Cathy her voice trembling read the notes aloud.

Malcolm had said the initial exploratory translation of his section of the papyri suggested that there was a maiden who lived in Lemnos when Philoctetes landed. A voice laughed in her head. Cathy clenched her fists. She thought, I'll start from the beginning - the beginning of *the Cypria*.

She tried to concentrate. It was difficult with the voices. Cathy desperately thought of something real, a name familiar to everybody, a real person in this crazy nightmare of disembodied voices, Brad-, Brad Pitt, now he had made a good job of bringing the story of the battle of Troy to the modern audience in his portrayal of Achilles in the film, even though pundits of classical literature considered the film version so altered from the original to be laughable.

Cathy thought hard of who it was that acted the role of Paris in the same film. I think it was Orlando Bloom, she said aloud, determined to override the noise in her mind. It all started with Paris. She read her notes out loud. Surely her voice would drown the ones in her mind.

Paris, the famous figure in Greek mythology who in the original story, *the Cypria*, written in the sixth century BCE, was the judge in the beauty contest between the goddesses Athena, Hera and Aphrodite. Paris judged Aphrodite to be the most beautiful and she being so pleased rewarded him with Helen the wife of Menalaus. This led to Paris raping Helen and taking her and her dowry back to Troy with him.

Menelaus, Helen's husband is consumed with rage when he discovers what has happened and asks his brother Agamemnon for assistance. Together they gather a great force and set sail for Troy to get Helen back. On the way they meet many adventures and calamities such as Agamemnon having to sacrifice his daughter by slaying her, because he had insulted the goddess of the hunt, Artemis. Agamemnon had offended Artemis by killing a deer and then boasting that he was a better archer than even the goddess of the hunt. Artemis vowed that unless he killed his daughter she would not allow safe passage for the ships on their way to Troy

After many episodes, including the story of Telephos, and the marooning of Philoctetes, the fleet leaves Aulis and lands at Troy. When the Greeks land, the Trojans' greatest warrior, Hector, kills Protesilaos, and the Greeks' greatest warrior, Achilles, kills Kyknos. The Greeks demand the return of Helen and her dowry, but the Trojans refuse. The Greeks besiege the city and *the Cypria* narrates the first nine years of that siege comparatively briefly.

Cathy stopped speaking. Tears rolled down her face. She had spoken so rapidly to cover the sounds in her head and whilst she was speaking the sounds had eased but now they were back just the same as before. Cathy put the book down.

She clutched her head and thought, 'What do I do? I must get help.' It was 4 a.m. Too early in the day to call anybody. She lay down on the bed and closed her eyes. She thought she was like something Matt had said, what was the word he'd used? Something like a channel, a conveyor of information between these two men who were carrying on a conversation in her mind.

A BLOODY CONDUIT!, that's the word, she almost yelled, sitting bolt upright in bed. If only she could understand what they were saying. Speak in English, Greek or Italian, French even..damn you. Damn that bastard, Matthew Mallard. It was his fault. He had ranted about some machine he'd developed. I could kill him. I'll tell the police.

    Cathy tossed and turned, getting more and more frustrated. It was nearly dawn when the voices eased and Cathy feel into a fitful sleep.

Chapter 13

Abdullah looked at the printout issuing from the machine. He glanced across at his friend. His friend had no idea what the machine was about. Abdullah had switched it on late last night. It was now early morning. It was Ramadan, the Muslim time of fasting and they were staying up late talking. During this month they would break their fast at sundown and eat a feast of special dishes, then they would stay up all night until just before dawn when they would fill their bellies before they renewed their fast. Afterward, they would catch up on their sleep.

This morning just before sun-up, they had consumed a hearty meal and conversation was now at a minimum. Abdullah's friend had to go. He said to Abdullah, 'I will see you tonight. I will bring you some more food. When are you going to get married and have your own cook?'

Abdullah said, 'I am a patriot of the North. I have a mission. When it is completed then I will consider marriage.'

His friend said, 'What is your mission? You have been very nervous tonight Abdel.' Abdullah remained silent

'You and your secrets. See you later.' The door closed.

Abdullah thought about how Istanbul was pleased at his acquiring the machine - Mallard hadn't had a clue, besides the hocus-pocus healer had been away- it had been a simple matter for Mehmet to acquire it and bring it back here to Northern Cyprus – 'People are so dumb,' thought Abdullah ---but not Al-din and Igor, their minds were as sharp as rapiers.

Knowing Igor, Abdullah felt sure there were plans already in place to use the machine on several of Al-din's enemies in Turkey. Why stop at enemies, business contracts could be won by programming certain thoughts in certain minds. It was a revolution in mind-control and Cathy Burkert was the vital ingredient for success, the Conduit, as Mallard had called her- IF they were able to succeed in controlling her. Abdullah knew the end-goal was Hektor Xanthis and the thought that he had Xanthis in his sights, that day in Xanthis' London office, when Abdullah had dumped the A/c unit, never to return - so close to the enemy, that he could have throttled the life out of him! Abdullah knew he would forever regret obeying the 'no-kill' orders from Istanbul.

Abdullah went across the room and read the last words on the printout. Cathy's last thoughts. She could not understand the Turkish language, but the machine actually worked. She could even hear background conversation- him and his friend talking just now.

What good fortune! Abdullah was excited. The possibilities were endless. He read the printout from the beginning. Allah, the woman was stressed!

He fiddled with the switches. He pressed all to the off position. First we have to get the machine working properly. There's parts of it missing, he thought. That stupid bastard Mehmet, I told him to take the whole lot from the Matt Mallard home. There must be an English decoder. I'm sure it was mentioned in the conversation in Burkert's flat. Fatima had sent him a copy of the tape. Where was it?

As he hunted for the tape, he glanced out of the window. How he loved coming back to his home in Kyrenia. It was April and the air was fresh and lovely. The mild winter had passed and the spring sunshine was gentle. A myriad of colour with daisies, poppies, wild tulips and anemones were to be seen on the fertile plains of the island. He turned back, rummaged a bit more and pulled the item out from under a magazine. He played back the tape.

'Yes. There is a decoder.' Mehmet would have to pay another visit to the good healer's surgery.

In the meantime here in Northern Cyprus to Abdullah's good fortune and plenty of bribes, he came to know of a Turk by the name of Salim, currently residing in Northern Cyprus, who had worked at the science institute in Canada attended by Matt Mallard.

Acting on Abdullah's instructions, Salim had phoned the institute and wasted no time in chatting up the secretary. He hailed her as a long lost friend and said that they had had many a conversation when he had worked there.

Although Gwen Miller the secretary could not place him she was happy to discuss Mallard with him.

Apparently Mallard had been in touch with the institute recently. That's why the secretary remembered him. He had asked for copies of the notes on the experiments conducted by the labs and a loan of the machine used. Gwen's bosses, scientists whom Mallard had worked with years ago, had agreed to the loan and Gwen the secretary grumbled to Salim that it had taken ages to package the bulky equipment.

Salim's brain had raced. He thought Abdullah had said that the machine was like a laptop, the integral part of which was designed to receive input from the mind, with a printer which spouted forth the printout, much like a fax machine. Not that bulky! Had the basic machine changed? No, was the answer. But the basic structure had been updated to include other functions.

And obviously since then, Mallard had added decoders and satellite receptors. Salim asked for copies of the notes on the machine's functions, used in the experiments and she agreed to fax them to him. Gwen thought it was all boring, mundane stuff of experimenting with cultures in the lab. She thought there was no harm in sharing data of experiments carried out a decade ago especially with an ex-researcher from the Institute.

There was a knock on Abdullah's door. 'Salim is nice and early, good' thought Abdullah. A few minutes later Salim was staring at the machine.

He said to Abdullah, 'Are you sure it works?

'Yes said Abdullah, Look I'll switch it on and show you. The printout will start to roll immediately. Her thoughts'

A couple of minutes later he said, 'She must be sleeping. The tape is blank'. He switched it off

Salim read the previous printout of last night. 'Mallard must have updated the machine, he added decoders'

'Yes as a matter of fact. He told Burkert so. The decoders are currently in transit, practically on their way here' 'We will adapt them to Turkish', said Abdullah with satisfaction. 'In the meantime, after you have had a chance to look at it we will keep it running just to receive Burkert's thoughts. We will wait for the decoders to arrive before we start inputting information. Our English is too poor to create the impression we want to!'

Salim remembered seeing Mallard in passing at the institute in Canada. Mallard had certainly been into some heavy stuff, he thought. Using his electrical energy to perform mind control. Of course in those days he had conducted experiments on organisms resulting in the said cultures achieving extraordinary growth in the lab.

And now he was trying his hand at other minds.

Abdullah told Salim that Mallard had told the girl it could only be done because the two of them were psychic and both possessed huge amounts of electrical energy. But Abdullah thought the good doctor was lying. He knew Mallard would need some form of electromagnetism- a computer that uses microwaves to deliver spoken messages directly to the human brain, as well as using radio waves to hypnotize people or change their thoughts, according to Igor's information from Istanbul. However, Mallard had withheld that information from Burkert, and he had certainly not confessed to the machine creating a hypnotic state in the victim's mind, when describing the machine to Burkert.

Salim now looked at the machine in front of him doubtfully. It didn't look as high-tech as he had imagined it would be.

'We could hook it up to satellites, our celestial friends,' he said aloud to Abdullah.

Abdullah slapped him on the back. 'Go to it comrade. Abdullah felt good about Salim's presence. Salim's expertise with computers and his connections to the Institute were precisely the reasons he had been hired.

To make doubly sure that Burkert got the message, Istanbul had suggested that Abdullah should be accompanied by a doctor when the machine was running properly, when it was time to co-erce Cathy Burkert mentally, not just any ordinary doctor but a man who knew how to take a human being to the limits of endurance. Mental endurance.

Abdullah stroked his beard. It was said that Dr. Hayat had learnt his trade from torturing the Kurds. Abdullah recalled the history of modern Turkey and the Kurds -The Treaty of Sevres signed by the Allies and the Ottoman Empire in 1920, after the first World War, did not allow as originally stated, for a separate Kurdish

State. The Kurds had rebelled over the decades and ways of stemming the uprisings had caused a need for Dr. Hayat's trade. Dr. Hayat – 'The Bitkisel' (The Vegetable-grower) as he was known in certain circles for his ability to induce a coma-like, vegetative state in his victims through mental torture.

Igor the Russian had sent parts he suggested might be compatible. Igor had suggested making a duplicate of the machine when Salim had it up and running. Ankara and the top brass in government, would be very grateful to have such a gizmo. Igor had actually laughed.

Now THAT thought Abdullah was an experience he would not like to have repeated. The strange strangled sound that sufficed for a laugh, had emitted from Igor's throat on the other end of the telephone and gave Abdullah pause.

Salim said, 'I will leave the machine switched off for a while in order to understand how it works. I might have to take it apart. Why don't you have a sleep, Abdullah? I'll wake you in a couple of hours.'

Cathy woke up with the telephone in the room ringing. It was her wake-up call. She groaned and clutched her head. There was no sound. The voices had gone. Had she imagined them last night. No, definitely not, she thought, I must get to a doctor when I get back. Determined not to dwell on it too much and feeling perfectly normal if a bit tired from lack of sleep, she got ready to go to the Department of Antiquities where she was meeting Malcolm and Tessa.

At the department Cathy got into work-mode straightaway. For today they would try and make sense of where the newly discovered papyri would fit into the story of *the Cypria*. Key names and words, iambic rhythms (rhythms created by words) would have to be examined. Laborious work but exciting too.

Shortly after lunch, a quick sandwich, Cathy's mobile rang. It was Hektor. Cathy thought, how lovely to hear his voice.

He asked, 'What are you doing today?

After telling him, he said, 'Will you be free for dinner?

Cathy said, 'I usually have dinner with Malcolm or Tessa the people I am with from the University but I'm sure I could get away.'

'I will call you later and let you know where,- it will be about eight, okay koukla?' Cathy felt a rush of pleasure at the endearment, she knew it was typically Cypriot and was a particularly affectionate term meaning, 'doll'. She agreed to the date, rang off and allowed herself the luxury of thinking about him whilst she accessed Homer's iambic rhythms on the computer.

It was one-thirty. Salim woke Abdullah. He said, 'I've finished with the machine. I think I know how it works. I'm off now to set the satellite link-up. Turkey needs to have access too. We should have touchdown in a couple of hours. I also intend to add the extras that Istanbul have sent- I believe your boss got them from a contact in the FSB, the bureau responsible for the internal security of Russia? By the way I switched the machine back on. It won't let any of *our* conversation through to her thought-stream, just her thoughts coming through. You might want to take a look at the printout that came through just now. It's all about a guy called Hektor......' Salim left the house.

Half an hour later Abdullah telephoned Istanbul. He was jubilant. 'Touchdown,' he said to Igor. 'The target has made contact with our pigeon. They plan to meet tonight. The printouts are full of her thoughts about him. Mehmet has texted me that the decoder is on the way. It was easy to get hold of. Mallard is out of the country. I should have it by this evening. Just one little hitch. Mallard said that whatever language Burkert thought in, it would be translated in English. With Salim's expertise and the hi-tech Russian extras sent by you, Igor we are hoping to add a couple of little variations, another channel possibly, including the necessary decoders and satellite hook-up. We hope to have part of it up and running by tonight. In time for the lovers' rendezvous.'

The Russian said, 'Good. Things are moving along satisfactorily. However, I suggest you step up surveillance. I realise you have a couple of men on the job but I want her hotel room taken care of. You know, install the usual video camera with the microchip which will bounce off the satellite to give us visuals and the audio equipment, both to be monitored from the van. And Abdullah get started on her brain straight after

Salim has added the attachments. Dr. Hayat will know how. Keep me posted.'

Igor switched off his phone and typed up his report. Al-din was away and had asked not to be disturbed, unless it was an emergency. But he was going to be very pleased with all the progress that had been made in his absence. Igor's hand smoothed the folder.

He glanced at the name on the top 'Mark Burkert, he said his voice soft and deadly.

Now what a fount of information that young man had been. And apparently it hadn't taken much to get him to talk. With such a weak head for alcohol and a hatred for his family – a family he hadn't seen in years and had no intention of seeing again, he was more than willing to divulge everything. Cathy Burkert's past all laid bare.' Well, well Dr Hayat would know exactly what to do with the information. Yes Nasr was going to be very pleased.

A short distance away from Abdullah's base of operations by the beautiful ancient harbour of Kyrenia, in a dusty little flat that the organisation used, the CIA man John Harper touched the top-secret file sent to his cell phone. Here he was in Northern Cyprus, part of his government initiative to make sure that all things went smoothly when the Turkish Cypriots voted the predicted 'yes in the referendum- however there was an attachment to an email he couldn't quite make sense of, he forwarded the 'e' to the main computer and switched it to blackout mode. The screen went black with a series of odd words. Harper pressed a button. The machine came alive with images and symbols. The decoder was set into motion.

'Cheerist!' he said whistling softly. He read the information quickly absorbing the details, last night's satellite monitoring at the US Secret Ops in Southern Cyprus, showed huge outputs of unexplained electrical energy- Target Location Hilton Hotel in Nicosia, Southern Cyprus- suspected Ascapitz in motion ----- – what the fuck was that? Access to a name- Bart Mellor and a phone number.

Harper picked up the phone and dialled the number – Somewhere in the sprawling campus of the Massachussets Institute of Technology, (MIT) a bearded youth held his cell phone to his ear. 'Just far enough away so as not to scramble his brains, he knew, man, what these things did to the old brain'- besides Harper sounded too loud as he was talking- 'Hold your horses I am up to my ears in Genome Research. I'll send you all the data – its getting close to being relevant to you guys down there.

Ascapitz? Yeah it rings a bell. I have a suspicion it might be classified – highly classified! Phew! Are you sure of your facts on this one? Details of Ascapitz on their way over as soon as I have them. And yeah, I'll try and find a satellite slot in the next hour or so- we are all booked up for now – Southern Cyprus-He spelt the word out loud N-I-C-O-S-I-A. Hang on I'll get the coordinates on the cell phone. Yep, you are now booked!'

Later that day, Bart Mellor flicked a switch on the machine in front of him. He had had to move mighty fast to get the necessary green light from the top brass. Mellor's job as an innocuous researcher at the Institute allowed him access to all the major developments in cutting-edge technology which he duly reported to his main employer- the man in the White House.

'This is MIT calling!' he said to John Harper. 'Did you get the 'e' on Genome Research and the package re: Ascapitz? Genome Research is Red hot and smokin' aint she? Gotta go into overdrive on that one stat. The other matter is different, here goes...Ascapitz occurs when there's a brain-drain via electronics, yep, key signature of the op. is a significant hike in electricity on the national grid, hence the power surge yesterday.

Alrighty, we are in possession of some intel from a monk called Papa Spiro from the Greek Orthodoxy- the wheels have been turning slowly on this one, don't want to cause any upheavals just now, but have a name from the Greek Papa, - a British citizen, a Matthew Mallard, and he too, has some curious electronic baggage.

The satellite link you asked for shows imaging of two, both male, individuals trailing Ascapitz victim. Initial profiles of the men indicate radicals of the Turkish Republic of Northern Cyprus. We believe they are the guys with the heavy machinery and the source of the upsurge - again refer Ascapitz -the word from your CIA guys, straight from the top is we hold back on this one, purely internal to Cyprus man, no action to be taken-- just a word of warning in the right ear– also Papa Spiro tells us, that the likely intended target is a Hektor Xanthis repeat Hektor Xanthis.

Xanthis is lobbying Uncle Sam for Armenian genocide- yep they think he's a prime mover and shaker in the Referendum too. Check out the 'Ascapitz' conduit- a female- Miz Cathy Burkert located in the Hilton – zooming in on CCTV images- for your eyes only on this one, sending details now-. Home in on your tracker! Coordinates are as follows...... I'm cueing you in as of now.

Mellor typed in the numbers and watched the image on the giant screen in front of him 'Babe, you got a great ass,' he said with an appreciative whistle.

Cathy walked out of the hotel, her senses heightened. She instinctively turned around and stared at the bearded man with what appeared to be a mobile phone held in front of him. Intuitively she guessed he was aiming it at her. Was he taking a photo of her? Cathy hurried, almost falling over in her haste to get to the waiting taxi. She was shivering, she kept staring behind through the rear windscreen to see if she was being followed. Was she being paranoid?

If she was being followed, who were they? Cathy was starting to home in all sorts of extra-sensory signals. Something was not quite right. Cathy tried not to feel a mounting sense of panic. Luckily, she was not going to the dinner date with Hektor this evening. He had called, was ever so sorry but had to reschedule till the following day. Cathy had at first been despondent at the cancellation but when Malcolm had suggested having dinner, with him and Tessa, in the old city of Nicosia she had agreed and her spirits had improved. Now, she scolded herself sternly to stop imagining things and enjoy the evening.

The CIA man in Kyrenia, John Harper, waited to receive the images from his man on the ground across the border in Nicosia. He stared at the screen and sifted through the images concentrating on the peripherals- Was that guy a face he should know or was he imagining stuff? A memory of the early days in Iraq- a face in the British contingent - MI6- hey buddy here's looking at you! Are we on the same trail? The scent of a woman? Harper grinned and filed his report.

Chapter 14

The following morning, Malcolm walked towards Cathy as she entered the building. He was beaming 'Thoroughly enjoyed the mezze meal last night and the Greek dancing- and of course the company' he said with a charming smile. 'Now I've got some exciting news,' he said 'I'm half-way through the Philoctetes section and I have uncovered an entirely new addition to the original tale. But first let's sit down.'

Cathy said, 'Malcolm I'll just get myself some coffee and I'll be with you'

Minutes later they were seated at Cathy's desk and Malcolm said, 'I've already briefed Tessa. Are you aware of the story of Philoctetes?'

Cathy said, 'No. I meant to ask you to enlighten me'

Malcolm looked like a schoolboy with a treasured secret. 'I'll tell you the story as far I have got. Philoctetes my dear, shot to fame because of Heracles. Let's go back a bit- you know the story of Heracles and his twelve labours?' At her nod he carried on, 'the labours he had to do to achieve immortality. Well, Heracles succeeded in all twelve labours and thereafter fought many a great battle. One day Heracles and his wife Deianira came to the river Evenis where the centaur (half- man and half-horse) Nessus, sat and ferried passengers across for hire. Heracles crossed over the river by himself but entrusted his wife to Nessus, the centaur, to carry over.

Nessus, the centaur, being a lecherous individual, violated Deianira in the journey across. Heracles heard his wife crying and shot Nessus in the heart with one of his arrows which carried the poison of the Hydra killed by Heracles years ago. Now Nessus was vengeful and with his last breath cleverly gave Deianira a love-charm mixed with the poisoned blood from his wound, saying this would bind her husband to her if he should ever stray.

Some time passed and Deianira suspected Heracles of having an affair so she used the love-charm that the centaur Nessus had given her. She sprinkled it on Heracles' battle-dress. Heracles wore the battle-dress and was immediately in agony. You see, Cathy, the so-called love charm was a poison that corroded the skin. There was no cure. Deianira seeing her husband's suffering increase, hanged herself whilst Heracles was told by the oracle to go Mt. Oeta where a huge funeral pyre was to be built for him.

And that brings our boy, Philoctetes, on the scene! For Heracles having abandoned all hope, ascended the pyre. And resting there, he asked everyone who passed by or came up to see him, to put a torch to the pyre. But no one wished to obey him, until Philoctetes came by. Philoctetes agreed to do the deed and received as a gift the bow and arrows of Heracles. That's how Philoctetes gained his fame all over the ancient world.

Malcolm looked at Cathy's green eyes filled with interest and caught himself wishing he was twenty years younger. He would have been quite happy to be the focus of such interest. The green eyes before him sparkled and glistened and for a moment he felt a long-forgotten passion for all things carnal. He blushed slightly at his thoughts and hastily carried on. 'Years after the death of Heracles, the seducer Paris came to Sparta and abducted, with or without her consent, Queen Helen, taking her to Troy. And because of this, a powerful coalition was formed of Achaean (Homer's collective name used for Greeks) leaders with a fleet and army gathered in Aulis in order to sail against Troy and claim Helen back. And among those who joined the coalition and fought in the Trojan War, was Philoctetes.

Philoctetes contributed with seven warships to the Achaean alliance, but he did not reach Troy until much later. For after putting to sea from Aulis, the Achaean army came to the island of Tenedos. There a number of unpleasant things took place. For Achilles killed King Tenes, disregarding his own mother, the goddess Thetis, who had warned him not to kill that king, or otherwise he would himself die by the hand of Apollo. So when Achilles, after losing his temper, had sent the king to his death, the Achaeans found it necessary to offer a sacrifice to Apollo in order to placate him.

And while they were offering to the god, a water-snake came out from the altar and bit Philoctetes. The wound caused by the snake proved to be incurable, and the stench which it produced was so difficult to endure that the commander-in-chief of the army, Agamemnon, decided to get rid of Philoctetes, putting him ashore in the island of Lemnos, where the fleet came after leaving Tenedos.'

Malcolm's voice abruptly came to a halt for Tessa had entered the room and appeared very agitated. Tessa spoke jerkily, 'Malcolm I appear to have mislaid all my notes. I cannot find them'. She wrung her hands and looked at him imploringly. 'I have searched everywhere and what's worse – Malcolm I don't know how to tell you this- The original pages of papyri were amongst the notes. What do I say to Andreas and the rest of the Cypriot team?'

Malcolm said, 'Tessa, calm down, first of all tell me how they came to be lost? Sit down, my dear.'

Tessa with a visible effort to be calm, sat down and began, 'Well yesterday afternoon, I was discussing with Andreas and a couple of others the translation I had done of the Leander pages. A couple of the paragraphs do not seem to make sense. I have grave doubts of the authenticity of the Leander, Malcolm -' Tessa turned to Cathy, 'I meant to include you in the discussion, Cathy but I understand you took a couple of hours off.' At Cathy's questioning look, Tessa said, 'Leander refers to your chap Morpheus almost exclusively with just a passing reference to Homer. Hence my doubts as regards their presence at the Homer recital'

Malcolm interrupted Tessa, 'You and Cathy can discuss the finer points later. What happened to the notes, Tessa?'

'Well I needed to clarify some things and I believed I might have copied the originals incorrectly so I asked Andreas if I could have another look at them.

Malcolm you know the Cypriots – they are so trusting – Andreas suggested as it was getting towards closing time that I should take them back with me to the hotel, and I'm ever so sorry Malcolm, I should have known better, but that's exactly what I did. I took them back to my room. And that's where they went missing! I swear they were in the room when I went to bed –

Malcolm said, 'Did you work on them last night?'

Tessa replied, 'No, I went downstairs for dinner with one of professors from the department and we spent rather a long time talking in the lounge afterward, with the result it got late and I was tired. So I went straight to bed'

At that instant, Cathy knew intuitively what had happened. The precious papers had been stolen. Cathy thought quickly – she could not voice her suspicions for in order to do so, she would also have to divulge that she had the ability for precognition, her sixth sense. They would doubt her sanity if she brought that into the equation. She decided to point them in what she knew to be the right direction, 'Tessa, they might have gone from the room whilst you were at dinner. For someone has certainly taken them. How else could they have disappeared? Have you spoken to the chambermaid? Perhaps she may have remembered seeing them when she turned your bed down for the night?'

Tessa said, 'Yes, that was my first thought too but no, the maid said she had no recollection of any papers. In fact, she seemed quite offended and was quite vehement in her denial, lest she was accused of throwing the papers away. That was not my intention – to accuse her but what else was I to think? Malcolm what do I tell Andreas? Those precious papyri, good heavens, the implications of such a loss.' Tessa sat looking devastated with tears rolling down her cheeks.

Malcolm took Tessa by the arm and said, 'Firstly we have to inform Andreas. I'm not sure if the police have to be informed as well - but that is presuming, they have indeed been stolen. Come, my dear.' His voice faded as they left the room. Cathy sat rigidly on the chair. She clenched her fists. She knew who the culprit was. The healer. He was here. She could sense his presence and what was far, far worse was that she could hear his voice at the back of her mind. She had heard it when Malcolm had been telling her the story of Philoctetes. It had been faint, barely discernible, as if from a great distance. Cathy had tried to dismiss it as her imagination, perhaps even a residue of the voices she had heard last night but no matter how hard she tried to override the healer's deep tones, she could still hear him, indistinguishable words, soft and deadly.

Cathy thought, 'So it's true. He did what he said he would. He's set up his machine with no physical presence required. He doesn't have to be here in the flesh to communicate with me. Had he also succeeded in the rest of his plans? What exactly had he said? Something about her healing people telepathically- that's it!- to tune into criminals' minds with the aid of some gadget and influence their thought processes before they committed harm.'

Cathy felt a sense of panic, 'How could she, a nonentity with no training of counselling, hope to influence criminal intent?'

The healer's voice answered, loud and clear, 'With my assistance! My dear Cathy, how nice to be with you in sunny Cyprus. Yes, I was true to my word. The whole thing is set up – a fait accompli. Now, now don't get into a tizz! I know I took your consent for granted but you are a decent sort of person. How could you possibly refuse to help people?'

Cathy said, 'I am here to do a job. I cannot have my mind invaded. For absolutely no reason, do you understand? No amount of moral blackmail will convince me that you are justified in penetrating my thoughts. I'm not having it. Go away!

The next instant Cathy was stunned when a different voice said, 'I agree the mind is a holy temple! But I believe in this case, Matt is right to ask for your assistance'

'Who is this? What's going on? Am I going mad?' stuttered Cathy, putting her hands to her head.

'Calm yourself Cathy. That is my friend Raji – Dr. Raji to you. (Raji, I'm switching you off for the mo.) He thinks he is talking to you, you know – umm, verbally. He believes this is a conference call. Raji is here to assist in a trial run. He has selected some patients of his, - they are paedophiles my dear, and have served their time in prison. They have been undergoing counselling for some time now and are due to rejoin society in the next few days. However, we want to make absolutely sure they do not re-offend. Dr. Raji has been the one monitoring them through their rehabilitation and when he realised (I informed him) that you have the power, through me and my machine -- uhh, to be truthful I didn't mention the machine. (We have to keep that secret for the time being.)

No, I said it was a natural phenomenon that both of us shared - That is true sweet Cathy we are natural telepathists. I told Raji that together, with our combined natural powers, we could influence other thought processes. He knows me by reputation, heard of my healing abilities, so he agreed enthusiastically to give it a go. Well here we are.'

Cathy said out loud, 'I won't do it. I have to work. I can't concentrate on my work with you in my head. My head aches already.'

Matt said softly, 'What a little fibber. Your head is fine and as for work – I believe I've taken care of that. Why, you will find that you may very well have some time on your hands because certain papers have gone missing. It was quite easy to gain access to the Prof's room when I overheard the conversation she was having downstairs in the hotel last night.' He laughed, 'So you have time now to perform acts of selflessness.'

Cathy said, 'I knew it was you. I knew you were responsible for the papyri going missing. Are you staying in the hotel? Have you been trying to tune into my mind using a foreign language? I've heard another language spoken. I don't understand it. I don't understand anything. What are you up to, you ...you devil,

'Cathy, calm down, you are probably picking up on voices in the region. Naturally, as I do. Do not be concerned -This machine can block out quite effectively your thoughts from shooting all over the place. Did you know that telepathy can be a two-edged sword- people's thoughts bounce into your head but yours can also bounce into other heads? Not to worry, I have taken care of that with a tiny little button called 'mute'. My dear, I will not tell you where I am staying. Suffice it to say I am close-by. No, Cathy you will not be able to inform anyone of this communication-- My dear, you are welcome to try. The beauty of this whole operation is that it is untraceable. Who would believe such a tale? Hush, Cathy we are wasting time. Raji is getting impatient. His patient is lying in front of him on the proverbial couch. The patient has a specialised microchip attached to the surface of his brain which connected to a computer enables my machine to access his thoughts and pass them on to you. You, as we both know do not need a machine!

Cathy, please try it out just once. See if you can make a difference to a person's life. Will you? I promise the papyri will make a reappearance once the task is accomplished.' Cathy could not think anymore. She felt hypnotised by the healer's voice. It was soft and persuasive. She could feel herself giving a nod of assent but she resisted. Desperately she sought for something to do, something to drown out the voices in her head. She must read something out loud. Last night, it had obscured the voices.

'Malcolm- the story of Philoctetes- where was he?' Cathy got up from the chair. It took a huge effort. She felt as if her feet were chained to the ground. She must find Malcolm.

The healer paid no attention to her movements. He was saying, 'I will introduce the first patient to you-remember Cathy- he cannot see you. Only his mind will be tuned in to yours. Your responses, you don't have to speak - just answer in your own mind and he will hear you. No, he will not hear you as a separate voice like you hear us. Your responses will appear to him as part of his own thinking process. Now do you see the genius of my invention?'

Cathy slammed the door of the room- hard and startled the secretary approaching her. 'Mr Malcolm has asked me to tell you that he and Mrs. Tessa have had to go with Dr. Andreas Michaelides to the police station to report the missing papers. He will telephone you later.' Cathy had difficulty understanding what the girl was saying. The healer's voice continued loud and clear. 'We won't tell you the patient's real name or the exact details of his crime. Let's just call him Bill. Suffice it to say that Dr. Raji is taking his mind back to how he felt after he had violated the child. Here goes Cathy -You are now in his mind'

The secretary stared at Cathy, 'Are you alright? You are shaking. Miss, miss can you hear me?'

Cathy did not answer. She almost ran, looking for the right door. A slow and ponderous voice in her mind kept time with her hurried footsteps, revealing details, disgusting details of an encounter with a child. Bill then recounted how at the start of the treatment he had been unrepentant, believing he could do nothing to change his pattern of behaviour - 'No mate. Believed it was the little hussy's fault. There she was looking so cute...'

Dr. Raji interjected hastily, 'And now'

'Yep, that was then, Doctor, now I am a changed man. I have seen the light' said Bill tritely.

Cathy reached the door of the room she was looking for- the Archive room. It also housed a collection of texts, both Ancient Greek and Latin.

'Cathy looked at the shelf – she had to read the rest of the story of Philoctetes. But, Cathy had begun to feel a glow that suffused her entire body. The electrical connection between her and Matt must account for it, she thought as her mind struggled to analyse it. Obviously the machine must enhance the natural energy. It was like a fever, a molten yellow fever. It was not unpleasurable in fact she could feel her pulse beating fast. Her entire body seemed to be consumed with liquid gold. Didn't Homer use the same description 'liquid gold' about the olive and its properties?, thought Cathy inconsequentially.

Dr. Raji's voice could be heard in her mind. He was saying, 'Bill, why do you feel as if you have changed? Do you still think you could do damage to a child- a fragile little creature, can you see how tiny she is?'

Cathy thought, No don't say that to him-that's what turns him on- the helplessness.

Bill said, 'That's what turned me on – the helplessness.'

Dr. Raji's voice, 'Bill you are analysing your behaviour. That's the first positive step to progress. Can you tell me anymore?'

Cathy thought involuntarily, 'Bill you are weak, your sickness makes you weak. It put you inside prison. You are helpless, just like the child you hurt'

Bill's voice said, 'Never thought of it that way before. But I ain't no pushover- helpless that I'm not - Hey doc, I'm a strong bloke – I'm no wishy-washy weakling.'

Cathy thought rapidly, 'You see Bill, because of your weakness, you too are open to abuse. Do not be weak. You must be strong and conquer your sickness. There is a way you can do this. I know you like butterflies, Bill. They are pretty and soft. Do your remember when you were a child you tried to tear one apart with your hands? Do you remember how you cried when it lay broken in front of you?

Bill started to cry, 'I wanted it to stay pretty. I didn't want it in pieces.' He had reverted to being a child.

'It could not fly anymore and you vowed to yourself that you would always treat a butterfly gently. You had forgotten that. From now on you will remember. Bill, every child is a butterfly. Whenever you see a child you will think of a butterfly'

Bill said, 'Every child is a butterfly. Don't hurt butterflies. Every child is a butterfly'

Dr. Raji voice was heard again 'We have made tremendous progress in this session. Matt, I've switched Bill off. I have to make some notes but if we can pick up again in an hour or two, I will have the next patient ready. Thank you both so much for this call. Miss Burkert has proved invaluable. I feel a tingling in my bones that we are on the very edge of a revolutionary cure for a diseased mind- Telepathic thought transport- Incredible! I have to tell my colleagues about this! Must publish a paper on the subject...'

Matt said, 'Catch up with you later, my old friend.' To Cathy he said, 'Well, well the good doctor is all fired up and with just cause. Did I not tell you we would make a tremendous team? Cathy, where the devil are you? I'm not receiving anything. Are you alright, Cathy?

The secretary, Maria, opened the door of the Archive Room. Miss Burkert hadn't looked too good earlier. She would just check to make sure – she paused and uttered an exclamation for Miss Burkert was on the floor, she lay crumpled in a heap, unconscious. The secretary rushed to get help.

Cathy woke up to ice-cold water being sprinkled on her face. She was sitting on a chair. For an instant her mind was clear. She had collapsed through sheer emotional upheaval. My God! She remembered what had transpired earlier, the electric glow and the feeling of supreme self-confidence and now – now she felt thoroughly ashamed that she had been unable to control her responses. She had literally been brainstormed. The healer and the Dr and the patient had taken over her mind and her responses to the situation had been automatic. She had been unable to think of anything else or switch off. Her mind had been totally and utterly invaded. It had been like a mental rape! But wait, someone was talking to her, there were faces staring at her, people from the Department- she must get up. Cathy stood up. She smiled weakly at them.

'I'm alright now. I feel better. I missed lunch today with all that's been going on, that probably why I fainted. Sorry for the trouble. I'll make my way back to the hotel. Could you please inform the Professor that I have left for the day?'

'Miss Burkert, the Professor has telephoned to say that he will be tied up for the next couple of hours with the enquiry into the missing papers. Perhaps if you leave a note for him at the reception of the hotel he will contact you when he gets back' said Maria the secretary, helpfully.

'Yes, said Cathy, yes I will do that.' Cathy glanced around at the Archive room and remembered what she had come for. 'First I need to get hold of a copy of the Philoctetes story and then I will be on my way. Thank you so much for your assistance', she smiled shakily at the secretary and said, 'I am perfectly well now.'

An hour later, Cathy had had a sandwich and was laying on the bed in her room. She felt worn out. She got up and walked to the mirror. Her eyes looked dazed and her skin was very pale. 'I want to look good for my date with Hektor tonight. Perhaps if I have a nap? She lay on the bed again and closed her eyes. The healer's voice said softly, 'No rest for you my dear. Not yet. Dr. Raji and I have been so thrilled with this morning's success that we thought we would try just one more patient today. Are you ready, Cathy?'

The healer did not wait for a response, he said, 'Let me give you a bit of background - This chap crossed in to the North of Cyprus on some business venture. The police arrested and incarcerated him, accusing him of being a spy. Obviously a case of mistaken identity as the poor man's family proved later.

Cathy, he was tortured with blows to his abdomen. He is so traumatised that he is a catatonic as a result – do you understand Cathy- he is in a trance-like state and cannot speak or eat or function normally. But we are going to reverse that. Are you ready?'

Cathy felt utter despair wash over her, 'No, no. no' she said out loud. She dashed up from the bed and got the copy of the Ancient text and feverishly thumbed the pages looking for the relevant passage.

Malcolm had said the Philoctetes had been put ashore on the island of Lemnos for the stench of the snake-bite could not be endured by the rest of the crew. Here it is. Cathy clutched the pages and read out loud, 'That is why Philoctetes, instead of fighting at Troy with the rest of the Achaeans, spent many years in Lemnos, using the deadly weapons he had received from Heracles , not to slay Trojans but to shoot birds in the wilderness which he turned into meals in order to survive. For the army abandoned him, setting out but a few rags, as though for a beggar, and leaving very little food. As he later recalls:

"For my stomach's needs this bow provided, bringing down doves on the wing. And whatever my string-sped arrow might strike, in pain I would crawl to it myself, dragging my wretched foot behind me."

Cathy paused and sank on to the bed. The healer's voice sounded – he was laughing softly, 'Cathy I cannot possibly have all sorts of Greek mythology, - mumbo-jumbo if you ask me - Now, now no need to feel superior because you are so erudite- yes my dear it does register, even the tiniest trace of a thought- I've switched Raji off by the way, not because you need a break- I am not kind when it comes to you Cathy – but because there is some interference on this connection. I think I should warn you that I have just been informed that certain bits of equipment have gone missing from my clinic in England.

At first, I had no cause for alarm as I thought it was common burglary. Besides, I felt sure the equipment was so specialised - and apart from the modifications I added, the basic machine is quite dated - No, having considered all, I did not believe that anybody would be able to fathom its uses. Unless- Unless, my sweet, you have told someone about the machine's function. What did you tell them?

Cathy said nothing.

Hmm, the feed-back I'm getting back from your thoughts is one of innocence. Yes, I agree that having been privy to all your thoughts I can be absolutely sure that you have not told anyone a damn thing. Cathy, the reason I am talking to you and I have turned up the volume - is to drown out other voices that have homed in to your mind at this very moment. The villains must have my missing equipment. I'm very upset that my equipment is being used by individuals whose credentials I am unaware of. I mean to get to the bottom of this. I'm sorry I cannot protect you – for the moment anyhow – you will have to put up with these hackers until I ascertain what the devil is going on! Adieu!

  Cathy had no time to absorb what the healer said for another voice said in her mind 'I am not getting a read-out. We have been talking for the last ten minutes but nothing is coming out of the printer. Are you sure you have configured it correctly?----- Is the radio frequency identity chip working? The one that will trigger the cameras installed in the room? Salim, turn that screen on. Ah yes we have visuals!
There she is the beautiful princess lying on her bed. This is such fun. Not only can I see you but I am in your mind. Abdullah nodded to Salim. 'We are getting

the read-out. It's working. Yes we are going to get very close, you and I Miss Catherine Burkert or may I call you Cathy? I think I will call you Cathy. Ah, are you going somewhere?

Cathy rushed from the bed. She held her hands to her head. 'Cameras. What cameras? She started to search the room wildly whilst the voice droned on in her head, commenting on her every move. It was a foreign voice, she was sure she had heard it before. 'Was it the voice speaking a foreign language from a couple of days ago? She couldn't understand it before but now the man was speaking English. He was laughing at her attempts to find what could look like cameras. He was saying 'You don't have any idea about this technology my dear. I suggest you go back to bed and stay calm while I tell you what is required of you. No, there is no use locking yourself in the bathroom. We can still see you.

Cathy started to panic. She rushed to the bathroom and shut the door. She crouched down on the floor hugging herself. How could they see her? How could they read her every thought just like the healer could? The healer had said they had stolen his machine. They could see her even now. How was that possible? How was she expected to relieve her body functions whilst in full view of the cameras? Why was this happening? What was she to do? She started moaning softly. The foreign voice answered, 'Cathy, Miss Burkert, get a hold of yourself. We need you to do something, something very small to you but of great importance to us. Go and lie down.

Take over Dr. Hayat.'

A soft male lisping voice said, 'I am a doctor Cathy. You needn't worry that I can see you even if you are naked'

Cathy squirmed and moaned, 'I have to tell somebody about this. I have to get help.' She got up and jerkily opened the door of the bathroom.

'I wouldn't do that if I were you. You see this communication is untraceable.' said the lisping voice

'I'll tell the police you are using a machine. Matt told me it's something to do with radio-waves' said Cathy aloud, her hand groping for her handbag and room key.

'I presume Matt is Matthew Mallard. Yes, he was most valuable. As for telling the police - Miss Burkert you are a representative of your country here in Cyprus. Do you really want to be taken for an insane creature? The police will ask for proof. What do you have to show them, apart from some wild claim of being watched and interfered with mentally. As to the first claim, the visual equipment will simply disappear but we really do not need to hide this machine. It will stay in this location. Believe me, it is truly untraceable. For, trust me, nobody knows about this technology nor is it within any realm of a normal imagination. Sit down. Please do not make a fool of yourself.

Ah I see you are starting to listen.' said the Doctor, watching Cathy slowly sink on to the side of the bed.

'What am I to do?" said Cathy in despair.
'Now, now there is no need to get melodramatic. This experience can be pleasurable. Shall I show you what I mean?' The voice became slow, hypnotic. Cathy lay down on the bed. Cathy felt her skin suddenly feel highly sensitised. Pleasure washed over her. The lisping voice was soft, barely audible 'I am like your lover. Can you see my face? It is Hektor. Hektor Xanthis.

'Hektor does not have a lisp' said Cathy weakly. She felt strange, disembodied. She could not move. Could a machine create a hypnotic trance?

'Indeed you are in a trance, but how astute of you. I forget you have the gift of precognition. Shall I put Hektor's voice on for you, Miss Burkert. Will that help you accept this communication?'

Cathy said, 'Please I know Mr. Xanthis only as an acquaintance, we are not lovers – I don't know what you are talking about' The next instant Cathy's skin crawled with distaste. She felt as if hundreds of needles were probing her delicate skin.

'As you see – pleasure and pain – I have the power to make you feel these sensations, and pain is what will happen Miss Burkert if you tell me lies.'

Cathy clenched her fists and lay rigid. 'I am not lying'

'I'll play your game for now. Hektor Xanthis is a very powerful man who is your lover. You are due to meet him this evening. We have been monitoring you so we know this with certainty. Now, my associates and I would very much like you to convey a message to Mr. Xanthis – on two issues, the lesser one is -we want him to desist from any involvement in the Referendum. The message he must put out to the public is promoting the Yes vote to reunification. Do you understand?'

The main issue however is the very important matter, and I cannot emphasise it enough - have you heard of the Armenians intention to use the term 'genocide' when they describe the events that took place during the First World War in Turkey? Let me tell you about how certain factions are trying to discredit this great nation of Turkey by insisting that we, the old Turkish people in the first World War, killed and maimed millions of Armenian people. It is not true, this is an absolute fabrication- we have a law about insulting Turkishness in our country. And this counts as the mother of all insults! It is not to be borne that your lover is inciting Washington to lobby for a bill to be brought before Congress proclaiming as a 'genocide' this private internal matter. Turkey is not responsible for these millions dying, their deaths and deportations were caused because they sided with Russia.

Cathy's body lay supine with the Doctor's soft words repeated over and over again. 'He's pressed the replay again and again, she thought. 'I feel no panic. Am I hypnotised?'

'You have an enquiring mind- hypnosis, you say? Well, lets just say it's a combination of several functions. I'm sorry to inform you that you will not be able to rise from that bed until I decide to release you. I can see you are trying very hard- its futile Miss

Burkert- unless you agree to do as I say you will not be able to move! I would suggest you stop struggling and recall the instructions I have given you. You must tell Hektor Xanthis that he needs to promote the yes vote to his people. More importantly, he must cease his contacts with Washington in the Armenian matter. Tell him that if he does not there will be consequences. Serious consequences. For you too. I have the power of life and death over you. I could spin your mind around until you are driven to your death.

 But wait- the readout of your thoughts shows you are defiant. Loyalty to Xanthis – a very useless trait, I have always found. Ah, but there is someone here with us who demands greater loyalty from you. Perhaps if I put your brother Harry on the line, so to speak, he will tell you why you need to change your mind. Talk, Harry, tell your sister that it is you.'

Cathy thought, 'It's not Harry. I don't believe in this communication. I must just lie still until it passes'

Harry's voice said, 'Cath it is me. Please do as he asks'

Cathy cried out aloud, 'Whoever you are, you are not my brother'

Dr. Hayat said, 'Harry tell her something that only you know about her' The lisping voice had a smirk in it. 'You know what I am talking about'

Cathy could see an impression of a face in her mind's eye. He was small and had thick glasses. Was this the doctor?' Somebody was sitting next to him. 'Was it really Harry?'

'Yes it is really your brother Harry. I understand that you have not seen him for a couple of years because his job as an airline pilot takes him all over the world. Luckily for us he had a layover in Ankara and we flew him to be here today. Miss Burkert, unlike you, your brother understands the need for Turkey to join the EU and indeed the sheer necessity of finding a solution between the Greek and Turkish Cypriots. Surely you too want the two to live in harmony'

'Of course I want that' said Cathy

'Well then it will not be a hardship to persuade your friend Xanthis to promote the yes vote to the Greek Cypriots'

'But the Annan plan is unfair to the Greek Cypriots.' said Cathy 'I was told that it gives too many concessions to the Turkish side. Isn't it true the negativity that exists is because the Greeks do not have access to their land since 1974, with little or no reparation for losing all their worldly goods and the psychological barrier of their rights being violated- the Turkish hit, grab and run syndrome?'

'Did Xanthis tell you that? Did he do that whilst he was in bed with you? Tell your brother and I about the man. Is he a good lover?' the doctor said with a leer. He laughed when Cathy flinched visibly.

'Cath, are you really intimate with this man Xanthis? Why Cath? I heard he's married' said Harry's voice.

'Hektor is an acquaintance, no more. I don't believe you are my brother Harry. I think these people have found some way of producing Harry's voice on the machine they have.' said Cathy to herself – loudly.

'OK Miss Burkert, I've tried the softly, softly approach. It's time for your brother to tell you exactly why it can't be anyone else but him. Do it' said the Doctor harshly.

'Sorry old girl, they have got me over a barrel. Reported for duty yesterday with rather too much alcohol in the system from the night before. Got found out when they did the pre-flight checks. They have promised not to let on to Management so I'm afraid I've got to do a bit of the dirty on you. Not so bad, really. It's only us here. The doctor has stepped out. Anyway, he wants me to remind you of the time you posed topless for money!'

'Harry, my god, it must be you. You were the only one who knew my secret. How could you, Harry?'

'No harm done Cath – only us! I did tell him that it was because you needed a large chunk of money for Mum to have private surgery and you needed it quickly'

'Harry you knew Mum needed the operation on her knee. The NHS doctors said the waiting list would take two years. She was in too much pain. I had to do it. My other modelling contract with the cosmetic company paid only my expenses at Uni. I needed the extra cash. But Harry, I told you- it was almost wrung out of me when I did tell you ...., therefore I can't believe you are doing this to me, you know that afterwards I was so consumed with hatred for myself. You know how much I've regretted doing what I did? Having pictures of my body plastered all over some magazine? Harry the only reason I confided in you was because I was absolutely disgusted with what I had done and I needed to talk to somebody. And now you've betrayed me you Judas!'

'Gosh Cath, that's a bit harsh.'

'I personally would like to wring your neck, young man' said the healer's voice.

'Matt. Thank God you are back. They have your machine Matt just like you said- but it's got some kind of hypnotic function to it because I couldn't move. I still can't.' Tears rolled involuntarily down Cathy's face. She made no attempt to wipe them away.

'Cathy I am very, very sorry about all of this. Apparently, they have made some modifications to the machine. They have added stuff that I've only heard talk about. Highly classified military intelligence stuff. No, Cathy I don't know who they are. I have my suspicions though- No, my love, I cannot do anything. They are too powerful. All I can do to help you is to talk to you – to try and block out their voices- I cannot stop them, I'm afraid, without exposing myself. They could get to me too because of my telepathic abilities just as they got to you. If they make any attempt to do so, they will not succeed - I've erected a wall of protection around me. It's too late to do that for you....

I don't have visuals of you but as I am still getting a print-out of all your thoughts, so I know that you are being watched. I also know from what is registering in your mind what your tormentors are asking of you. For the mo, they can see you but can't get through to you. Mainly because I am talking to you. I'll bet they are not getting any print-out of your thoughts either. I've switched you to 'mute'. They don't know about my set-up here. They believe they have the only machine that can do this to you.

That's why, my dear, I am able to help you by talking over them. There will be certain times when I have to rest but I plan to enlist others to help when I am unable to be in attendance. People I can trust. No. not Dr Raji and his patients- You couldn't cope with the stress- just some of my family who I will have to confide in. No doubt they will be absolutely shocked by what this machine does and will look at my actions with disgust but I still believe that what we have together is worth it. We are the only two in the world sweetest Cathy - and having been steeped in the paranormal world all my life, I know how valuable our communication is.

No, my dear, I can't let you talk at the moment. I have to block out the others. Whilst I have been talking to you I have been trying to tune in to their frequency and although it's not very clear, some stuff is filtering through. At present they have your brother repeating again and again your teenage folly of posing naked. I will address that issue in a mo. - I see these bastards intentions. Cathy they have a trained individual at work here. He knows how to apply the pain and pleasure principle to make you do his bidding. My God, this is the stuff of trained interrogators. But why you? They have gone to considerable expense just to get you to convince Xanthis – hmm I wonder who the devil is behind all of this and why! Sure, the Armenian genocide is a weighty matter, and these chaps belong to an extremist faction that take the issue of insulting Turkishness seriously. There must be moderates though- let me try and contact a few people and see if I can sound them out.

Cathy I didn't want to force you into an admission about Hektor Xanthis. I wanted it to come voluntarily from you. Yes I have known about him. I made sure I found out everything there is to know about the man. Speak quickly! Now are you due to meet him this evening?'

The tears had made the pillow wet. Cathy moved her head and that took a great effort. Her head felt heavy.

'Good. You have some movement. Because they have not been able to reach you the hypnosis is wearing off. Now to my earlier question. Are you due to meet Xanthis?'

'No. I'm not.'

'You are lying to me Cathy. I cannot help you if you lie to me. I know he is your lover and that you and he have had a relationship for some time now. Xanthis is a very powerful, very rich man – my Cypriot sources tell me he is tipped to be the next president- are you important to him? Is that why these people are targeting you? If Xanthis knew about this infiltration of your mind, would he protect you as I'm doing? Would he, Cathy care at all? You are after all just a lady friend! He has several so I'm told. That hurts doesn't it. You are not going to cry again are you?

Cathy If I told you that I'm so bloody jealous that it twists me up inside at the thought of you and him – my god I never thought I could feel so murderous of another human being - but …But- I do understand your need to have him in your life. It's all to do with your childhood and your father. It's the classic case of the older, father figure-someone as rich as Croesus to give you that cushion, that guarantee of financial security, should you need it. I know you think you love him but

I wonder if you had to make a choice between him and I, whom would you choose? And I promise you that there will come a time, very soon, when I will ask you to make that choice.

By the way, the villains who have stolen my equipment are getting frustrated that they are unable to get a readout of your thoughts. They keep on fiddling with all the knobs – yes I can hear them - what's this? I feel sure they are going to override me in a moment- the mute switch is proving ineffective. They are talking of playing a tape made by another member of your family, oh my dear, they found out about your brother Mark. They intend to torment you with your childhood fear and loathing of him touching you. I know their purpose. They mean to make you malleable to their wishes by reducing your self-confidence to such an extent that you are quivering mass of guilt and fear. Hey, whoa steady on girl- Cathy don't be afraid, lovely,

I will hold them off, but I cannot talk forever. I need to set up a rota with my family taking over at intervals. I have to leave you, to do that, but before I go off the air so to speak.....

I want to address the issue about you posing topless. I will just say a few brief sentences about it and I want you to remember it should they attack you with it again – my dear we are living in an age where exposure of the body is not a crime. Why on the beaches in the Med. and elsewhere women go around topless and half-naked. Nobody thinks any the worse of them for it. I realise with your Catholic upbringing you would feel terrible about it but honestly Cathy think back to your childhood - your actions in posing topless were a direct result of your brother touching your breasts and the helplessness it engendered. Therefore when an opportunity occurred as an adult, you asserted a measure of control over your own body, you made the decision to bare those bones and my lovely girl, you did not realise that the guilt from when you were touched by your brother, made you turn your body into a weapon, what you considered, an instrument of self-harm.'

'I did it to help my Mum'

'Yes but the reason you beat yourself up about it all these years is because for you, it was such a big sin to pose topless. Do you think yourself a bad person because of it? Did you think you were a bad person because your brother touched your breasts? I think you did. These people who are intent on destroying your spirit know all your secrets. They will succeed in destroying you if you are consumed with guilt. You must never think you were bad. You were not the aggressor. Your brother Mark was. He was the root cause of your self-hatred.

Do you see, my dear? So, put an end to this- nothing to feel guilty or ashamed about. I must leave you now - the others, they are playing the tape. It is your brother Mark reminding you of the beating he gave you - Cathy, get up. Come on now, do something, get up and move about, don't stay still – read your Greek story. Don't let them get to you with the hypnosis routine. I promise you I will be back soon armed with some of my own tapes- soothing music I think.

And Cathy I suggest you do not keep your date with Xanthis this evening. You might be tempted to tell him what is going on. If you do he will drop you so fast putting as much distance as possible between you and him. I, my little wanton, would like nothing better but you, I suspect would be bereft! Take care!

Chapter 15

For just a moment there was quiet in Cathy's mind. She immediately got out of the bed and went to use the bathroom. Before the thought could form in her mind, the hated lisping voice sounded again Dr Hayat– 'Yes I can see you. You are using the toilet. I can also see you are acutely embarrassed. So much the better. Perhaps now you will be open to suggestions- ah but you are still showing defiance in your thoughts- no matter. We are most interested to know why we were unable to get a read-out of your thoughts for over a couple of hours. What happened Miss Burkert? Abdullah and I could see you staring at the ceiling but nothing appeared in the print-out.'

Cathy gulped – she could not stop her thoughts.

'The healer was talking to me but this time I wasn't a conduit' She bit her lip hard as she realised what she had revealed - this could make things very hard for her.

'Talking to you? But there was nobody in the room. And what is this conduit? I haven't been informed of this.' Harsh laughter then sounded. 'Your mind is an open book – well, well so Mallard must be using another device. He has got hold of another machine. Is he in Cyprus, Miss Burkert?

I will find out you know'

Cathy tasted blood on her lip where her teeth had chewed so hard. She could not stem her thoughts. The lisping voice said,

'I see you believe that he is near. Does he know about us?' The voice was deadly, soft.

Cathy jerked. The telephone in the room was ringing. She rushed out of the bathroom and picked up the receiver. She tried to speak but her voice would not emerge.

Malcolm's voice said, 'Cathy is that you? Hello Hello.'

Cathy struggled, cleared her throat and stuttered, 'Malcolm yes it's me'

Dr. Hayat's voice said in her mind, 'You cannot tell the professor anything. He will think you are crazy. You cannot reveal details of the mission that is required of you- you remember- you have to convince Xanthis! If you tell the Professor about us, you will have to mention your liaison with Xanthis. If the public found out that Xanthis, the next president of Cyprus, a highly respected married man was conducting an affair with you, it would be an utter scandal. Don't forget, Miss, that Cyprus is practically governed by the Orthodox Church- they would never tolerate such an affair. Xanthis would lose the nomination. Do you want that?'

Malcolm was saying, 'Got your note at reception. Cathy are you alright? Your voice sounds incredibly distant. I heard what happened to you earlier- fainting in the department.. Are you unwell? I was going to suggest we meet downstairs in about half an hour so I can bring you up to speed on events. Do you feel up to it?'

Cathy said hurriedly, trying desperately to keep her voice calm, 'I'm fine. I'll see you downstairs in thirty minutes.' She put the phone down grabbed the hairbrush off the dressing table and ran it through the long black hair. Almost falling over herself she grabbed her handbag, mobile and room key and went out of the room. The lisping voice followed her, warning her to keep silent, down the corridor and during the lift's descent to the ground floor.

Cathy took a seat in the plush seating area. The wrought-iron chairs clad in orange velvet were cushioned and soft. Cathy thought through every detail of the simple act of sitting down. She had to override the lisping voice with her own thoughts because God help her Harry was talking to her again about the photographer who shot the topless poses. She squirmed in her seat as he recounted that the man had made her make dance movements to get the best angles. Cathy stared through the tall glass windows with a haunted look. Her eyes could see the swimming pool and people swimming - if only someone could help her-but who would believe her, how could she prove that this machine existed?

She stared at her mobile. The next instant she pressed the numbers quickly. The minder's voice answered. 'I have to speak to Mr. Xanthis.' whispered Cathy

'He is in a meeting at the moment but he will call you back'

'Thank you' said Cathy. She switched the phone off.

Cathy ordered a cup of Greek coffee. Harry's voice had stopped for a precious few minutes. 'Were they loading another tape?'

Just then, Malcolm took the seat across from her and with a concerned look, said: 'Cathy you look incredibly pale. Are you sure you are alright?'

Cathy nodded feeling tears of weakness and self-pity start to her eyes. She blinked rapidly and heard another voice in her mind. This time it was her brother Mark's voice. He was talking about their father, recalling all those beatings and days of shame in their youth when the creditors would come to the door of their house.

Cathy burst into speech talking quickly. 'Malcolm what is happening regarding the investigation? Maria the secretary at the Department of Antiquities said that you had to file a report at the police station.' Cathy did not dare mention any outside influence at this stage- she could not say that she knew who had taken them. Had the healer got the chambermaid to actually do the deed of pilfering the papers or had he done the job himself?

Malcolm said, 'Yes. The police plan to question the chambermaid when she comes on duty tomorrow. CCTV in the corridor shows that she was the only one to enter the room after Tessa had left to go downstairs. They feel she must know something. Cathy, we have to suspend our work at the moment. Tessa, you see, discovered before the papers went walkabout, that there might be huge discrepancies in the Leander account – you remember the whole basis of proof lies in the accounts written by both Leander and Morpheus of being present at Homer's recital of the *Iliad* and the *Odyssey* -Proof that will proclaim Homer as the definitive author of those books. Well, Tessa's news is disappointing. Her findings suggest that Leander wrote of Morpheus doing a rendition of Homer, rather than Homer himself performing. How did you do with the Morpheus account?'

Cathy felt grateful for Malcolm's presence. She spoke with knowledge and certainty. As she described in detail her untutored findings she felt her confidence returning. Above all, she was able to drown out Mark's voice in her mind. 'Obviously, Malcolm, you and Tessa will need to verify my efforts but initially I believe that Morpheus did attend a recital by Homer and then recounted what he had heard to his friends, including Leander,' concluded Cathy

'That is positive indeed. Give me your notes and I shall go over them. As I said earlier we have to find the missing papyri before we can proceed collectively. The Department understands that and has told us to stay here for as long as it takes so if you wanted to do a bit of touring around Cyprus, you could very well take a couple of days off, my dear.'

Cathy said hurriedly, 'Malcolm I really would like to work. I need to concentrate on something.'

'No need to be so diligent, Cathy, relax and enjoy the country. These are exciting days for Cyprus with the referendum looming in the next few days'

Cathy turned her head to hide the look of dread on her face. She thought of the pressure she was under to get to Hektor and warn him about the referendum and the Armenian issue 'Dear God' thought Cathy.

She needed to keep Malcolm there talking to her. She needed to drown out that voice. The voice, her brother Mark's, was still talking about their father and the memories it invoked made her feel helpless and dejected. The healer had said that is what these villains hoped to accomplish – to beat her into submission so that she could carry out their wishes. She must *not* see Hektor tonight, she decided. She said to Malcolm,

'Malcolm are you free for dinner this evening? I thought we could continue the discussion on Philoctetes. We got interrupted this morning'

'I would like nothing better than to tell you where I have got to on old Philly, Cathy. It's now 5 p.m. Lets meet at seven in the bar.' Malcolm left with a casual wave.

Cathy's phone rang. It was Hektor. Cathy said, 'Hektor I am unwell. I cannot see you this evening.'

'What is wrong, koukla?'

'Oh Hektor I really want to be with you but I must not see you,'

'*Must* not? Strange words.'

'No, no I meant I cannot because I may be starting a cold and I don't want to pass on my germs. I just need to rest.'

'I see. Alright I will call you tomorrow to see how you are. I hope you will be better.'

Hektor rang off with a few endearments. 'He's lovely', thought Cathy 'but I must not see him whilst I am under duress. If only somebody could help me! Please God. Where was Matt? He had promised he would return.'

The lisping voice said in her mind, 'There is no help out there. You have made things even more difficult for yourself now. If you had given the message to Xanthis tonight you would have been left alone. But, you have a misguided sense of loyalty. No – there is no point in feeling protective of Xanthis. Bismillah- you are a strange one! Xanthis is quite capable of looking after himself! Catherine Burkert I suggest you go back to your room for there is no rest for you until you do as we ask!'

Cathy signed the receipt for the coffee and hurried to the room. It never occurred to her to demand a change of room. Her mind seemed lost, completely subjugated by the hypnotic stream of harsh language. She desperately felt the need for privacy and she needed to lie down.

'If only she could think clearly without the hated voices in her mind' but there was no let up.

Cathy got to her room and lay on the bed, in a benumbed state. She longed for some peace and quiet of mind. But it was hopeless. Cathy didn't know how long she could carry on for before screaming aloud. She felt so ill. She felt unable to move again.

The voices, grimly familiar by now constantly repeated her failings creating scenarios where she was always found wanting. She would respond because her mind knew no other way. Then came the threats of imminent harm and death to both her and Xanthis' family. Always was their need to communicate the urgency to Xanthis- the urgency to desist from the Armenain genocide and the referendum! The repetition constantly created a kind of fever in her mind. One of harsh, corrosive electricity, rough and abrasive no more romantically Homer, no more molten, liquid gold of Homer's olive- just a wiry hair-shirt. She believed she was going to die.

Cathy lurched out of the bed. She must get help. The phone rang. A voice said, 'Cathy are you ok?'

Cathy said 'Hello?'

The voice said, 'Its Malcolm, Cathy. I have been waiting for half-an-hour. It's now 7.30. Did you forget? Are you unwell?'

Cathy steadied herself, 'Malcolm, I shall be down straight away. Sorry! Sorry!' She put the phone down.

Cathy felt dazed, disorientated. She must tell Malcolm. She must get help. Cathy looked for the metal door key. It was twisted and bent out of shape. A new voice jeered in her mind. 'Well, well are you trying to prove your ability for telekinesis? So what, eh Cathy to have such a talent- a spoon-bender-the ability to open doors without a key- bloody laughable! Will you attempt to bend the lock later?'

Cathy took the stairs. The voice now was English but it wasn't Matt's. 'No, I'm Matt's brother and I had my arm twisted to take over talking to you. Matt said to play soothing music but I thought I would use this opportunity to tell you what I think of you- Matt filled us in on the details of your predicament. I don't believe you are as innocent as Matt says. Personally, I think you are a scheming hussy. Carrying on with a President-elect. A man years older than you.

But he's rich isn't he? Of course that's the attraction, isn't it?'

Cathy said nothing in her mind. She had reached the ground floor and saw Malcolm waiting in front of the lifts. She went towards him and together they entered the restaurant. Cathy was not hungry but forced herself to eat the delicious Stifado, a Greek dish of stewed beef in red wine and onions. Malcolm did most of the talking during the meal. Cathy said very little. At one point Malcolm had to repeat what he said a couple of times.

Cathy could not concentrate. Matt's brother, Jim, had started to introduce other members of the family to her and they were conducting a conversation between themselves around the machine which meant that Cathy heard every word they said to each other.

Cathy was furious and the anger helped bring her out of the hypnosis induced by the brainwashing earlier. She thought rapidly and angrily, 'Matt said his family would stop the others from talking to me but it is still an invasion of my mind - this is no better than the brainwashing! Fuck off all of you. Just leave me alone. Don't talk at all anymore. I have had enough'

Malcolm said, 'Shall we have coffee in the lounge? We can continue the Philly saga. I have finished all of the translation' He tapped the briefcase he was holding. 'It is fascinating and one of the fragments indicates a new discovery.' He took Cathy by the arm and led her to a sofa.

Cathy was deliberately not paying any attention to the voices in her head. To cries of 'Shame on you. We are only here to help. Matt insisted we were to talk to you to keep the wolves at bay. Would you like us to unleash the dark side of the force instead?' Male laughter and hysterical giggles from a woman were heard in Cathy's mind. They obviously did not understand the severity of her situation. Despite Matt's instructions they thought it was all a bit of a caper, more than likely Cathy was crying wolf and appealing to Matt's inner calling to protect lame ducks- that much was obvious from the conversation in Cathy's mind. She concentrated fiercely on Malcolm's words, determined to shut them out if she could.

Malcolm said, 'I marked the page where we got to- Philoctetes had been put ashore on the island of Lemnos for the stench of the snake-bite could not be endured by the rest of the crew.'

Malcolm's eyes gleamed, 'Now my dear, the rest of the story as the world knows it. That is until this discovery! But first let me tell you the official version. You see, the tale was that Philly spent many lonely years in Lemnos while the rest of the Achaean fleet were fighting at Troy. As time went by, the difficulties of the Achaeans in the war were at least as hard as the solitude of Philoctetes. For many years passed and Troy could not be taken. So in the tenth year, the seer Calchas declared that the city would be taken if the Achaeans had the bow and arrows of Heracles fighting on their side. Others have said that this prophecy was uttered by the Trojan seer Helenus when he was captured by Odysseus. Not too important who uttered the portend actually-

Suffice it to say, when what had been prophesied was known to all, the Achaeans sent Odysseus and Diomedes to fetch the bow and arrows from Philly, which they did, either through persuasion or by force. Furthermore, the embassy of Odysseus and Diomedes in some way or another accomplished its mission of getting not just the weapons – you know Heracles' bow and the arrows, but Philoctetes himself to join the fight at Troy,

Philoctetes' greatest achievement in the war was the shooting of Paris, who died a painful death because of Philoctetes' poisoned arrow. After the war, Philoctetes was among those who were dispersed by the naval disaster at Cape Caphareus. He then reached home at Meliboea in northern Hellas, but having been expelled by a sedition, he emigrated to Campania in Italy. There he fought the Lucanians, settling finally in Crimissa, in the southern part of the country, where he founded a sanctuary of Apollo, to whom he dedicated his famous bow. The death of Philoctetes has not been reported.'

Cathy's mind was bemused with all the names and places mentioned by the scholarly Malcolm. 'He was so knowledgeable,' thought Cathy. 'although a bit heavy-going' She was grateful, however, she had been so absorbed in the story, the voices had been a faint murmur in the background. 'If only they could be controlled all the time.' She must find a way!

She said, 'Malcolm, what is the new development? Your excitement is palpable.'

'There was just one fragment in the papyri discovered here in Cyprus and the reason we are here, Cathy, just ten lines- but, boy, it has added a whole new dimension to the story. The original story had Philly spending all those years in Lemnos on his own with some reports stating that he was helped by the Lemnian shepherd Iphimacus.

My papyri indicate that this was not true- that he was helped by a maiden- a beautiful young girl- she was one of the priestesses in the Temple and she helped to heal him. Not by the sons of Asclepius as was previously thought but by Halcyone, priestess in the Temple of Apollo'

Cathy still looked bemused. Malcolm looked sharply at her, 'Cathy you do not look suitably impressed. Don't you understand that this offers Greek mythology experts a whole new slant on the story? For Odysseus when he came to enlist Philly's aid in fighting in the Trojan War, must have had to use guile to persuade him.

There has always been a doubt as to how Odysseus persuaded Philly to fight for a side that had abandoned him when he, Philly was in terrible pain- Yes almost definitely Odysseus would have had to use cunning especially since the fragment states that Halcyone the priestess had cured Philly. You see, Philly had no reason to go back with Odysseus. His wound was cured. His needs were taken care of by the beautiful Halcyone-

Cathy, I have undertaken some further research whilst the search for the other fragments of papyri is under way. I intend to find out what means of persuasion were used by Odysseus to get Philly back on the Achaean side'. Seeing her faraway look, he said, 'Humph, Concentration is not your strong point this evening. You look decidedly peaked. Take a couple of days off. Go to Paphos. Didn't you tell me that's your favourite place in Cyprus?'

Cathy thought for a second. She said, 'Yes I will, Malcolm. I will take a couple of days off. I'll arrange it first thing in the morning'

Ten minutes later, she had said goodbye to Malcolm with a promise to ring him in a couple of day's time. Cathy hurried up to her room. The voices of the Turkish faction had returned with a vengeance. Obviously Matt's brother Jim had better things to do than to override the Turkish channel. Cathy did not have the key to the room. Her stress had resulted in it being mangled. She would have to go downstairs to reception to ask somebody to let her in.

The man in the van, young Mehmet, picked up her movements through the CCTV cameras in the hotel. He watched the beautiful girl walk down the corridor and wait for the lift. She was holding her head in her hands.

He made a call to Abdullah. 'The pressure has been non-stop for a couple of days. I think she is showing signs of cracking. What is Hayat's view?'

Abdullah said, 'Difficult to say. Hayat has been surprised at the level of resistance he is encountering. She seems to have an iron will. Will not get in touch with Xanthis- cancelled the date she had. Moreover, she plans to go to Paphos for a couple of days. Leaving tomorrow- we thought that might be a problem with the machine but Salim has set up another satellite link there so we should be alright. Also, the printout of her thoughts indicates that Xanthis plans to call her tomorrow. We must ensure she warns him during the call. Time is running out.'

The voice answered,'Igor has ordered us to increase the pressure tenfold! We have to get results in the next couple of days. The tide of feeling amongst the Greek Cypriots must change – there are clear indications that they are going to return a 'no' vote. Istanbul is getting very restless at the lack of results. We must succeed'

'I'll do my best, said Abdullah. 'Possibly arrange a little accident- a reminder, to show Miss Burkert how deadly serious we are.'

Chapter 16

The hated lisp dominated Cathy's movements while preparing for bed. She heard the words trailing through her mind over and over and the worst thing, the very worst thing was that she would respond. God please help me. Her mind was drowning in memories of the bad times in her life. Tears started to Cathy's eyes. She was exhausted. 'Where was the healer? She needed to speak to him. Cathy cried softly.

Cathy did not sleep that night. The Doctor played his tapes and for hours- all about her father's failures, his debtors- he explored her feelings of shame, he dwelt on them for what seemed like hours, creating a burning acrid sensation in Cathy's stomach. Cathy felt utterly defeated. Having got her at such a low ebb, Cathy then heard nothing but his voice's insistence of her talking to Hektor Xanthis. On one occasion 'Talk to Hektor or you will be sorry. Very sorry. Do you want to go over the edge of reason? We could help you to do exactly that! Your behaviour will affect your mother, your brother's flying career, your sister Fiona's children –what are their names?'

Cathy would respond, 'Carol and baby Ben. Please don't hurt them.'

'We don't want to Miss but you must see that Xanthis cannot go to Washington to meet with the Armenian lobby. Secondly, he must promote the yes vote.' This was the kinder voice. His name was Abdullah. He told her he didn't mind her knowing his name because there was no way that anybody would believe her story.

Abdullah would, in his words, create fields of energy by using a certain switch on the machine that would cause her to shiver all over with pleasure. Then he would talk to her softly, persuasively, how much he admired her - for her beauty and for her intelligence. He knew that she loved Xanthis but because of her love for him, she must warn Xanthis that he was at extreme risk of harm coming to him or his family.

He knew the men he, Abdullah worked for, they were ruthless. Xanthis or his family would be harmed. Just tell him. No more, no less.

'I cannot. I will not give in to coercion' said Cathy. And so the torture went on hour after hour.

It was a very long night. Cathy got out of bed at 7. She was mentally spent. She decided to take a taxi to Paphos as she did not dare risk driving in her state. She would hire a car to get about when she was there. She washed and packed a bag, went downstairs and gulped down a cup of coffee whilst waiting for the taxi.

Two hours later she was heading towards Paphos on the old Limassol road. She hadn't been this way on her previous trips. The taxi was approaching a bend in the road and Cathy caught her first glimpse of what must be one of the natural wonders of the world. The view expanded the closer they got and Cathy feasted her eyes on the huge sweep of the bay with its now turquoise, then a bit further aquamarine, and then again deeply blue swathes– a necklace of gemstones- how she loved this banquet of nature. A fitting birthplace for the goddess Aphrodite with the waves foaming around the distinctive rocks. Cathy could picture the goddess treading the ocean, nubile and incandescent.

Then they were heading for Paphos and Cathy asked the taxi driver to drop her off at the picturesque harbour with all its cafes and restaurants. She walked along the quayside breathing in the sea-air and watched the boats. She started to feel a faint stirring of hope despite the disturbance in her mind. Even though this time the disturbance was not threatening.

Matt's relatives had taken over. They had assumed control on the journey down from Nicosia. Matt Mallard had made adjustments, (so the relatives informed her) and now they didn't need to group around the one machine. Each one in different parts of the country had been supplied with a voice box and basically they could talk to each other without having to dial a number or be connected in any other way. 'And Matt says- it's to do with global systems and positioning and that it's all because of your amazing abilities! Your mind and Matt's machine has made this happen. Matt says that your output of electrical energy has increased a thousandfold because you are under such tremendous stress.' said his brother Jim

'Don't feel like a football being kicked around dear' said an elderly aunt.

'It's just that some of the family haven't seen each other for yonks' added a younger cousin 'that's why we love to talk for ages. Besides, that what we are here for – to keep the bad guys off this frequency'

Cathy had given up explaining that it was of no help- that the constant talk in her brain produced a kind of fever, a hypnosis, regardless of whether it was from friendly or hostile forces. They could not hear her. Only Matt and the Turkish element got hold of the print-outs of her thoughts.

She dipped her hand in the sea-water by the walls of the old castle in Papohs harbour and brushed the wet hand across her forehead. She would stop at a cafe in a minute, have a medium Cyprus coffee – a metrio-and then would hire a car. She had bought a Cyprus tourist book of places of interest and she planned to visit some of the sites. Could she manage to, in her state of mind, she wondered?

'I must. I must. I cannot let them get to me.'

By mid-afternoon, Cathy was getting weary. She had visited the ancient site of the House of

Dionysos by the harbour, then the Tombs of the Kings and with the hire car had driven to Latchi, north of Paphos, passing unspoilt villages on the way. In Latchi, she had stopped for a fish lunch in the lovely little harbour. Cathy ate mechanically, barely tasting the delicious food in front of her.

After lunch she visited the Baths of Aphrodite and dipped her fingers in the shaded pool. It was the Italian poet, Arioste, so she was informed by Matt's aunt Leila, who named the natural spring from which Aphrodite also used to bathe- the Fontana Amorosa. However you needed a four-wheel drive to get to the spring. Here at the Baths, the water was velvet green in the pool of the natural grotto. The fig-tree above the pool introduced muted rays of the spring sunshine and she thought of the legend, that to take a sip from the ancient sacred site would be a promise of love to come. Cathy cupped her hand and swallowed a few droplets. She needed that promise to come true.

Cathy's mental outlook improved during her tours. The English voices in her mind were talking desultorily amongst themselves- they were not threatening or demanding. Cathy began to be lulled into a false sense of security. She liked, in particular, Matt's favourite aunt, Leila, who talked knowledgeably about Cyprus. She knew all the places Cathy visited and had comments to make about each. Cathy like hearing about the fabled area around the Fontana Amorosa, made famous by medieval classical writers, even though many had never visited the place. Leila recited a verse from one such poet, Arioste: 'And in truth, every woman, every girl is more pleasing there then anywhere else in the world; and the goddess makes them all burn with love, old and young until their last hours'- Cathy listened bemusedly to the musical tones and felt much better. Besides, being out and about in the fresh air had certainly helped and the sunshine was glorious. The voices in her mind whilst still there, seemed to be coming from a distance. She could cope with that. She wondered if the machines could only be used within certain ranges- Cathy quickly dismissed any thoughts associated with machines and mind-games.

For on the drive back to the hotel in Paphos, at the forefront of her mind a burning question had arisen. Had the Turkish lot succeeded in brainwashing her? Because a thought had occurred, and now recurring incessantly, was beginning to be a conviction!

Was she being foolish not to warn Hektor? Should she take the threats being made against her and Hektor seriously? Trouble was the threats were being made only in her mind- Not aloud. How could she convey a warning of something that existed only in her mind? Cathy thought long and hard. For when she was harangued by the voices constantly she could not think clearly. Now that the voices were somewhat muted, common sense and more importantly her psychic abilities reasserted itself. She was certain that something bad was going to happen. To Hektor!

If she did warn Hektor, he would want to know where her information had come from. He would consider her mentally deranged if she told him she had heard it in her mind. She could not even mention that she was psychic because he knew nothing of that side of her. She had kept it secret from everybody. Only the healer knew and of course now the evil contingent from Turkey!

Cathy checked in to the hotel. It was located by the harbour within easy walking distance of the bars and restaurants. Cathy thought it would be nice to wander down there later. She went up to the room with a plan that when Hektor rang she would intimate that he might be advised to be careful. She could not say anything else! Certainly nothing about voices threatening her! While she knew that he wouldn't ridicule her he would suggest she went to see a doctor. And that's the last thing she needed. They would certainly commit her! Cathy picked up her mobile- perhaps she should not wait to receive a call from Hektor-perhaps she should ring him NOW!

    Cathy picked up her phone and pressed the buttons.

    Hektor's minder answered. Hektor was away for a few days. He would be given the message that she had called on his return. Cathy suddenly felt terribly alone.

With that thought her relative peace was shattered as the voices picked up momentum. Abdullah and Dr. Hayat and a woman. She said her name was Fatima, brought in from London. 'I am your nemesis, the one who compiled the report on Mallard, when I first heard him speaking in your flat. You hate me now but wait till I tell you more.....Well, to begin with it's all hands to the deck for the next few days' said Fatima. 'Are you feeling a sense of importance, my dear? Don't! You pitiful creature! Because you are about to discover that we have done the unthinkable. We have cloned the machine!

We got encouragement when your thoughts revealed that Mallard had set up another base using you as a conduit to conduct healing therapies- what a load of crap you're into Burkert, By the way, he won't be able to get through to you anymore. We have managed to over-ride him! Anyway, our man worked on it all last night and here we are. I am here in Paphos whilst Abdullah is in the North and Dr Hayat is off to Turkey to set up a unit there. So you see, you will be like a football, being kicked around- because we plan to use your mind as a conduit- with a second channel- to get to our enemies. We tried to do it without you being aware but it only works if I talk to you (or play the tapes) on the one channel while on the other, thoughts are floated through. No, you will not be able to know what is being said on the latter channel. I am about to test the system we have set up. You poor bitch! But hey Burkert, some consolation, you are indispensable!'

The next instant Cathy heard the old tapes playing of her childhood and her father's debtors – stopping Hektor in the referendum, stopping him meeting the Armenian lobby over and over with ever-increasing insistence but wait! there seemed to be voices speaking above the tape, through a separate channel in her mind- she could not distinguish words – they were in a foreign language but they were causing her to feel very ill.

The Turks had obviously created another channel through which they could talk without her understanding the content of their speech. The woman Fatima had said that they were trying to influence their enemies and using her mind to escape detection.

Fatima's voice said shrilly, 'You are very very clever, Missy. Yes it is as you say but the beauty of it is that we speak and your mind conveys the message to the intended target- as a thought in their minds- no more. A form of auto-suggestion using you as a conduit. The targets do not suspect a thing.'

Cathy felt very ill indeed. The pressure on her brain was intense. She did not get up from the bed all evening whilst the voices raged on in her mind. During the course of the evening Dr. Hayat's voice joined the cacophony and he kept up the pressure throwing little switches on the machine which induced pain and pleasure. Her phone rang twice but she was unable to hear it. Dinner time came and went and Cathy laid on the bed fully clothed with tears pouring down her cheeks. At midnight Cathy crept to the bathroom unsteadily.

She was dazed and disorientated. She cried for the healer but he could not hear her. 'Was he still getting print-outs of her thoughts? Did he know what was happening to her? He had said they were the only two in the world who could communicate telepathically. Could she do it- find a way of overriding all the outside interference and get a message to him?'

The Turkish voices laughed and jeered at her attempts to formulate a means of escape. Cathy laid on the bed and stared at the ceiling. She would wait for an opportunity. She went into a fitful doze.

Two hours later Fatima paused to make a call on her progress with Catherine Burkert. Igor for once did not answer. Fatima did not have Al-din's private number. It was late in the night and the office was shut. Strange, thought Fatima, for Igor not to answer his mobile. Normally he was always on call.

Igor, had Fatima, or worse still, had his cousin Al-din known it, was spending another sleepless night after betraying his cousin and master. Igor's loyalties had been divided as soon as he heard about Hektor Xanthis' support for the Armenians.

Whilst Igor was quite happy to support Nasr's attempts to manipulate Hektor Xanthis on the Referendum matter, Igor withdrew his tacit agreement to prevent Xanthis from lobbying for US support of the Armenian genocide. A genocide that Igor's grandfather had lived through and died for. No, thought Igor irrationally, Nasr could not expect Igor to compromise his own beliefs and his Armenian birthright – although, of course Igor knew full-well that Nasr had no knowledge of Igor's Armenian heritage. But then Igor was not thinking straight. His mind greedily absorbed the nuggets of information he could gather about Xanthis' meeting with the American Armenians. He decided to precipitate matters.

Three days ago through his contacts in Washington, he got to know of whom Xanthis was meeting and when. It was a simple matter to re-schedule the meeting by bringing it forward by ten days, and acting on Igor's advice, the American Armenians suggested to Xanthis to keep the revised date to himself. Xanthis had agreed and was even now returning to Cyprus, having been closeted with the influential core of the Armenian movement for the better part of a day. According to the Armenian in Washington, Igor's contact, the meeting had been highly successful.

Let Abdullah and Fatima and the doctor carry on at Burkert as if nothing had happened, as if Xanthis was still a deadly threat to Al-din and the Turkish extremists. Igor would issue further instructions to them in the morning. Suspicion could never be placed at Igor's door.

Igor for the first time in his life felt his grandfather and his father would have been proud of him.

Cathy jerked suddenly. There was a moment of quiet. They must have been loading a tape. This was what she had been waiting for. She curled into a foetal position and with every fibre of her being tried to get through to the healer. 'This is an SOS Matt.' Quickly she told him of the different machines and the different locations. 'Help me please Matt' The voices started again.

5 a.m. Cathy blinked at the clock. She suddenly sat up full of resolve. She tidied herself, took her overnight bag and went downstairs. She had

trouble waking up the night receptionist. The man was not pleased at her request. Nevertheless he allowed her to check out of the hotel. Cathy got into the hire car and started the drive back to Nicosia. She would telephone the car hire company and ask them to pick up the car from Nicosia.

Cathy knew what she had to do. Somehow with all the noise in her mind Matt had managed to get through. With a sense of utter conviction Cathy knew that it was Matt who had put the idea in her mind. Matt was unable to help her anymore. She must gather up her courage despite the brainwashing. Cathy must go to the British Embassy and tell them everything! She was heading back to Nicosia to do exactly that! Cathy would, she decided get back to the hotel in Nicosia and find out where the embassy was. She reckoned she would arrive there just as it opened for the day.

The next instant the car's bonnet flew up and smashed into the windscreen and the car careened into the side of the road. Cathy slumped over the wheel.

Chapter 17

The motorist in the passing car saw Cathy's vehicle laying skewiff on the hard shoulder. He pulled up in front of the car checking the situation in his windscreen mirror. He could not see the driver of the stricken vehicle because the bonnet was flush against the windscreen and was obscuring his view. He got out of his own vehicle and hurried to help. The girl inside looked unconscious, her head was slumped to one side, there was no sign of blood or injury.

He spoke to her asking if she was alright and could she hear him? There was no response. He hurried to his car returning with a bottle of water. He could see her stirring.

Cathy opened her eyes and lifted her head. There was a man talking to her. His face was vaguely familiar. He held out a bottle of water and said her name. How did he know her name? Cathy took the bottle and sipped gratefully. He was saying something to her in Greek, asking if she was alright. Cathy had difficulty replying. She was listening to the voices in her mind.

The voice in her head was exultant. Fatima said, 'We warned you that an accident would befall you, didn't we, kaltak (whore)? Do you believe this to be true now? I can see that you do. Go back to Nicosia and get in touch with Xanthis. Tell him what you have been instructed to do.'

The Greek man was now examining the great crack on the windscreen. 'Where had she met him before?' He was saying still in Greek, 'Cathy do you remember me? I know you understand me. I remember that you speak Greek. My name is Stelios. We met in London a couple of years ago. I was with Hektor Xanthis. I remembered those eyes - as soon as you opened them, I recognised your face straight-away'

Cathy stared at him whilst registering his words- the turmoil in her mind combined with the shock of the accident made it difficult to concentrate. She clutched his arm and blurted out, 'They are trying to kill me.'

Stelios looked at her and said, 'What is this? Who is trying to kill you?'

After a pause of silence, a whole pregnant minute while Cathy gathered her wits and then blurted hastily, 'I'm sorry-it's not true- the shock of the accident –I don't know what I'm saying'

His eyes probed hers. He said 'Are you sure?' Cathy said more confidently this time, 'I'm absolutely sure! My mind was just playing tricks' She forced a short laugh.

Stelios carried on talking in Greek saying that she was probably in shock after the incident and that she should not drive the vehicle anymore.

Cathy said in English. 'I will be alright'. She got out of the car and watched him test the bonnet several times ensuring it stayed shut. Stelios was still talking in Greek. The voices in her mind were too loud for her to comprehend his words fully, but she did recall the face in front of her. She had definitely met him before. From what he was saying, Cathy gathered that he was expressing his puzzlement at the reason the bonnet had flown up as there appeared to be nothing wrong with the catch.

'Luckily the glass remained intact and did not fall back into the car, you could have had a serious injury. Did you not shut the bonnet properly?' he said.

Cathy answered with a slight impatience 'As you can see by the red number plates it's a hire car - I had no reason to open the bonnet.' 'No need to check oil and water, she added in explanation

Stelios said, 'Where are you headed?'

She answered, ' I'm on my way to Nicosia'

He said, 'That's where I am going. Look let me give you a lift and I will arrange for the hire company to collect the car. It is too dangerous with that great spiderweb crack. You can barely see out of it.'

Cathy shook her head and said, 'There is no traffic at this time in the morning. It is imperative I get to Nicosia. I have an appointment to keep. There is just enough space for me to see out of the screen. I will be O.K.'

Cathy firmly shook her head at his renewed offers of assistance. She consented to giving him her mobile number so that he could call her to make sure that she arrived in Nicosia safely, but Cathy with dogged determination said thank you and goodbye. All the while Fatima, the banshee, continued her evil dialogue in Cathy's mind.

Cathy double checked that the bonnet was closed, the bonnet, she was certain, whose catch had been deliberately loosened to enable it to crash back into the windscreen with such force causing the damage to the windscreen. She felt a moment of sheer panic at the thought of being persecuted but in the next instant she thought, 'Stiff upper lip, Burkert!' She got behind the wheel of the car. There was a small area in the windscreen that she could still see through to drive. She drove off.

Cathy parked in front of the hotel in Nicosia. It was now 8am. Cathy thanked God for getting her back in one piece. She was shaking with reaction as she almost fell out of the car. The voices in her head had been strident throughout the journey. Also her vision had been affected. She kept on seeing patches of red. Probably as a result of the accident, thought Cathy, clinging on to some shred of composure. She felt like screaming aloud. She thought of calling Hektor to hear his voice. A voice so dear to her. He loved her in his way. He would provide a degree of comfort in this awful nightmare, but it was too early in the day to call him.

Upstairs in her room Cathy showered and changed her clothes. She knew she was being watched and listened to. The voices ran on unabated, operating on two different channels in her mind. On one the tapes played and the other was a channel for conversations in a foreign tongue. Turkish – she was beginning to recognise it. Cathy dried her hair and stared blindly at the mirror.

Like an automaton, she went out of the door. Cathy spoke to the receptionist who made markings on the map. Cathy got into the car. People were about now and were staring at the car. Curious looks directed at the crack in the windscreen. She drove out of the hotel.

Cathy steered the car out of the exit and joined the busy lane of traffic. She hoped she wouldn't be stopped by the police for driving with a damaged windscreen.

Suddenly, Cathy felt calmer because Matt was with her. She couldn't hear him but she sensed his presence like a wall around her, protecting her. He was communicating somehow.

The voices now howled rage and threats of imminent death in her mind. Cathy was undeterred. The shadows under her eyes from tension and lack of her sleep were very dark but Cathy had never looked more beautiful. She checked the name of the street. Archbishop Makarios Avenue. Not far to go. The traffic was heavy at this time in the morning and would have normally bothered Cathy but she was oblivious to it. She drove forward inching her way along – she saw Cyprus Airways on the left and knew she was heading in the right direction.

Meanwhile Stelios - Xanthis' right-hand man who Cathy had encountered when she had her accident earlier in the day was obeying instructions from his boss. He was following Cathy as she made her way through the rush-hour traffic. Stelios after recognising Cathy had helplessly watched her drive off despite his remonstrations that she should take it easy, had phoned Hektor even though he knew he would be disturbing Hektor in his strict morning routine of exercise in the gym before the start of the working day.

Hektor had said, 'This had better be good. I've just returned from a long-haul trip' On hearing what Stelios had to say and asking a few pertinent questions, Hektor had insisted that Stelios drop whatever he had intended to do and follow Cathy posthaste. 'Report back to me' said Hektor 'I am very concerned'

Hektor had switched the phone off and instead of going back to the private gym in his modest mansion—modest indeed for a man of such means— had drifted to the poolside where he pulled out a chair and thought long and hard about Cathy Burkert.

Hektor was used to women fawning over him. He was not unattractive and his wealth and power attracted the dolly birds in plenty. What was it about this particular one? He could not remember feeling so smitten since he was a youth. Sure she was young and beautiful but -there was something- something pure about her. She wouldn't accept any of the trinkets and favours he bestowed on the others. She was proud and stood alone making her way in the world. Hektor decided that the attraction must be her vulnerability- it brought about his protective instincts- he decided he would have to take extra care of her. Hopefully Stelios would report back soon!

Hektor put Cathy to the back of his mind and went about his busy schedule. The referendum was only a couple of days away. Hektor felt his own lobbying of people in the corridors of power aiding their own individual assessment, was beginning to take effect. The Greek Cypriots were starting to form a consensus that the Annan plan for reunification was not in their favour. Even his good friend, the President, Tassos Papadoupolos had made an emotional speech to the nation a few days ago, calling on Greek Cypriots to reject the Annan plan.

Hektor knew that the US and the UK governments were applying significant pressure on the Republic of Cyprus government to accept the last-minute Turkish demands, simply to get an agreement on the Cyprus issue.

An agreement on Cyprus was a major goal of the US Administration but it became clear that the Turkish General Staff and Denktash, the leader of Northern Cyprus, a Turkish puppet backed by the Turkish army, continued to rely on the US to apply pressure on the Republic of Cyprus Government.

The latter, the Greek Cypriot Government of President Papdopoulos had in their stead, relied on Washington's indications that it was applying pressure on Ankara. The US seemed to be playing both sides against the middle.

Hektor knew that the Annan plan would cement the division of Cyprus into two political entities and safeguard the presence of settlers in the North from mainland Turkey, both of which were felt to be illegitimate and unfair outcomes. Hektor felt vindicated for his negative stance on the whole issue.

Besides the Annan plan on re-unification, the other highly secret issue currently on the table and known only to a few in the top echelon of Greek Cypriot government circles, was to actively encourage and support the labelling of the Armenian genocide by the US- it would certainly throw a spanner in the works between Turkey and the US. Hektor felt satisfied with the progress made to date and with his whistle-stop trip to Washington to meet the Armenian lobby, which had gone exceedingly well.

Hektor was also cheered by the news, that MI5 no longer believed that his entire shipping corporation was under threat from terrorist activity. All relevant ports had been under high-alert but further threats of a deliberate oil-spill had not materialised and Hektor had begun to breathe easier. Now, Hektor thought that it was obviously the work of a lone 'nutter'- MI5 had reported that trail had gone cold in Northern Cyprus and Hektor felt thankful that was an end to the matter.

However, despite the positive feeling he had, there was an item of disquieting news. Something very disturbing had come to his notice from government security services- a name he hadn't heard for a couple of years – Nasr Al-din- what's more in connection with some nefarious activities- possible monitoring of individuals in Cyprus??

He had asked to be briefed in full and had a meeting set up with the security services later that morning. They knew of his childhood association with Al-din and were keen to get even the smallest nugget of information. What the devil was Al-din doing in his neck of the woods?

The last he had heard of him was a photograph in the newspapers with the story that he was involved with high-level talks with the Turkish government- something to do with natural resources- gas and energy. In the world that Hektor moved in, notable individuals within the Northern Cyprus and the Turkish hierarchy were known to Cypriot government sources and Hektor had heard via the grapevine Al-din's name being mentioned from time to time.

Hektor had listened with interest to the stories involving his old playmate Nasr Al-din - Stories of corporate achievements, an ever-increasing portfolio of business interests. Hektor had wished him well and had reflected how both of them had made their fortunes, from humble origins, each in different ways.

But this was a change of focus for Al-din- this current alleged interference within the Republic of Cyprus was a very grave matter. Hektor shrugged mentally, he would find out more soon enough. He headed for his office.

The man whom Hektor Xanthis had briefly dwelt upon would have been overjoyed to have caused Xanthis even a moment of concern. Years of hating Xanthis had turned into a phobia, a disease that infected Al-din's psyche. Al-din knew that the only cure for his malaise would be for Xanthis to die or to be severely humiliated. Utterly ground into the dirt! Better than death! Instead, living proof for him, Al-din to witness!

Nasr summoned Igor. Time to get an update of the situation.

Half an hour later, Nasr was being escorted by Igor to an unfrequented and unused part of his office building. He noticed one of his men was positioned at the end of the corridor, standing guard. He uttered his approval to Igor. He entered the room and saw the array of machinery positioned on the table. Nasr's knowledge of electronics was limited so he had no idea of how the thing worked, his sole interest was witnessing personally this incredible connection that had been established through the English girl's mind- what a bloody great find she had been- and his targets here in Turkey. Things were starting to happen. Ministers who had ridiculed him were starting to make friendly noises.

Just this morning, the minister for energy had phoned him, Nasr, totally out of the blue. For two years Nasr had been trying to set up a meeting with the minister in connection with his application for acquiring stock in the pipeline and the bastard had kept avoiding him.

But yesterday a whisper had floated into the minister's mind. A mere hint of a thought at first- that Al-din could be an asset. Oddly enough the thought had kept recurring to the minister throughout the day. The minister decided to meet Al-din to sound him out and had telephoned Nasr to set up a meeting. Other people, business contacts, were making moves- positive moves - Nasr smiled wolfishly.

He said to Igor, 'So this is it.'

He indicated a switch on what appeared to be a screen and said 'What does this do?'

Igor pressed the switch and replied, 'See for yourself'

The next instant the screen lit up and a room appeared – a hotel room. 'Is this the girl's?' asked Al-din

'Yes' said Igor 'She's obviously not there. Do you want me to find out where she is?'

'No' Nasr pointed to the printout spilling forth continuously, 'What's this?'

'Those are the thoughts going through her head- yes every one of them'

Al-din looked at him, 'Do you mean to say even the ones we have introduced? Does she know what we are saying to people here?' Al-din's voice sounded ominous.

Igor explained hurriedly about the two channels they had created. He said, 'We believe that Burkert hears us speaking but cannot understand what we are saying. In any case, there is no need to worry because what is she going to do with the information? Who would believe such a thing exists?' Igor laughed and Al-din felt a chill. He had always hated Igor's laugh.

'You had better be right. You my friend, have nothing to lose. I, on the other hand- 'He shook his fist at Igor. 'What is happening about Hektor Xanthis? In light of recent events with Burkert being so useful as a mental conduit-the necessity of getting to Xanthis is almost redundant – but persist with it nevertheless, I want to see that bastard is fucked up a bit!'

Al-din turned to the door, 'Don't push Burkert too hard. She is proving very useful for now, with the creation of the second channel. She is like gold dust, with her psychokinetic abilities, without which, as you said earlier Igor, we would not be able to get to the minds of others- machine or no machine! We don't want her going over the edge. Tell Abdullah immediately.'

As he turned to the door Igor said, 'Cousin Nasr, I have to tell you of a new development, one which will please you greatly. The meeting between Xanthis and the Armenian contingent in Washington is delayed Sir. I have prevailed upon our contacts in Washington to delay the meeting indefinitely. In the meantime, you Sir will have no trouble anymore in gathering support here for bringing Hektor Xanthis down. I have bought us some time! (Igor lied without a trace of culpability, knowing full well that the meeting had already taken place)

Al-din beamed at Igor, 'Is this information accurate?

At Igor's nod, he said 'Firstly feed it through Burkert's mind to the right parties. Just a whisper of a thought to the right individuals. We will stoke them up initially with just the thought of the outrage to be perpetrated on Turkey by Xanthis and his Cypriot backers (I already have two key people in the government on my side). Keep floating the thoughts through Burkert's second channel.

- and then - and then my Russian cousin, I shall address the issue openly to each. They will be more than willing to help us get rid of Xanthis, as the matter would have been on their minds!

I believe we have the perfect reason for moving our operations into the Republic of Cyprus from the North. Key people in the government will facilitate entry. Goodbye Hektor Xanthis' Al-din laughed and cocked thumb and forefinger in the motion of shooting a gun. He said, 'Speaking of the CIA, we would not want to upset our American pezevenk's (sonsofbitches). Are you sure we are undetectable? I am concerned!'

Al-din had he but known it should have been extremely concerned - For, the CIA man John Harper had put a trace on the Northern Cyprus contingent-

Washington had suggested that he do it with the utmost caution, their pro-Turkish policy in the region was at stake. Harper had managed, with a few favours and a promise of sharing of information with the Greek Cypriots, routed the trace within their neck of the woods. He had discovered plenty, and whichever way you looked at it the trail led to a mainland Turkish base. One man's name kept on coming up, a Northern Turkish Cypriot, a Nasr Al-din- with links right to the top of Turkish government circles. Washington would have to have a word in the right ear.

The Greek Cypriots would have to be informed. Harper had a name at covert operations- Black Stallion. He picked up the phone.

Igor in his turn was on the phone to Abdullah. He relayed Al-din's instructions of treading carefully with Cathy Burkert. 'Where is she at the moment? She is not in her room'

He listened for a few minutes. 'Where is she heading to? You don't know? Nothing in the printout? Has Mallard set up another firewall? Hang on let me check the printout on this machine- It will take me a few minutes. I'll call you back'

Cathy gripped the steering wheel and glanced in her rearview mirror. She was being followed. Was it the grey car behind her? Or was it the silver one two cars behind? Didn't they leave a space of a couple of cars, as in the movies? She had long suspected she was being followed, but now – now it had been confirmed. Confirmed by the voices in her head.

For Cathy had heard every word that had been spoken by the two men. Not just heard but understood the Turkish being spoken. 'Matt's done it! He's managed to install another convertor. I knew he would find a way of helping me'

Who were these people? A lot of absolute bastards were using her mind as a conduit –to transmit messages as thoughts...vermin! A man called Igor and another – Igor's boss-- for Igor had called him Sir- Had she missed hearing his name? Cathy could not remember. They had mentioned Hektor. How did they know Hektor? She must listen hard for the boss' name. If she had a name she could have something definite to tell the British Embassy and also concrete evidence to warn Hektor!

Cathy drove on, peering through the cracked windscreen, listening intently.

Chapter 18

Stelios was two cars behind Cathy. He watched her take the turn first right after the cinema, 'Where was she headed to? He made the turn and then he couldn't see her car anymore. Had she made another turn? He looked again and with relief saw her car had pulled in to a petrol station. He drove a little ahead and pulled in to wait on the opposite side of the road.. But what was this?

Another car had pulled in behind him, an old green Mercedes. Stelios checked the occupants out in his rear-view mirror. A burly looking man was driving with another male passenger. Both men's heads had turned and were looking towards Cathy's car. Stelios became curious, 'What's going on?' He suddenly remembered Cathy's words of someone trying to kill her- she had dismissed it shortly afterword putting her admission down to being a result of shock after the car accident and Stelios had believed her but now... He saw Cathy come out of the petrol station with what appeared to be a map clutched in her hand. She was getting in behind the wheel.

Stelios decided to wait and see if the green Mercedes with the two male occupants, showing such an interest, would follow her. Cathy was turning around back the way she had come. 'Bingo, said Stelios aloud, for the green Merc had turned around and slotted behind Cathy's car. Stelios waited for a break in the traffic to turn his car around. But the rush-hour stream of vehicles held him up- he fretted, cursing under his breath and three minutes later was past the traffic lights with the general hospital on his left and desperately trying to spot Cathy's car and the green Merc but there was no sign of either car.

Stelios decided to check the roads leading off, but there were so many bloody probables!

Half-an-hour later, Stelios came to the conclusion that they had turned off somewhere. Stelios turned back. Stelios scratched his head, 'What to do?' -

Something was niggling at the back of his mind- her possible destination- what was around here that she was making a beeline for? He must find her or Hektor would be furious- especially when he told him about the suspicious green Mercedes following Cathy. Stelios decided to call Hektor and inform him immediately about the car. These were fraught times especially for

Hektor-best he was kept in the know ASAP. Stelios made the call.

Hektor was unavailable. Stelios called Hektor's secretary- she informed him that Hektor was in a meeting and could not be disturbed. All Stelios could do was to leave a message for Hektor to call back urgently. Then Stelios remembered he had Cathy's mobile phone number. She had reluctantly given it to him after the accident. He filched out the piece of paper from his pocket and punched the buttons. Cathy's phone just rang and rang. Stelios started to feel anxious. 'Where was she?'

Hektor meanwhile was reading intently the contents of a file. The man sitting opposite him was a powerfully built man with iron-grey hair. Hektor looked up. 'Is this true? I can hardly believe that Al-din is involved. Why would he have an interest in my movements? You say you picked up indications a year ago? Why was I not informed earlier?

'If we had told you, Hektor, you would have tried to take matters into your own hands and we would have lost the connection to him. By keeping an eye on his men here, and watching their movements, and thanks to our informants in the North and indeed

Turkey and some interested parties (the Americans have confirmed what we long suspected)– we are now able to say that, yes, he is definitely the head honcho of the motley crew - and what's more he is gunning for you, my friend.'

'Why me? I haven't seen him since I was a boy?'

'Let me tell you a story. We managed to piece together events going back to 1974- back to the last time you saw Al-din'.

For the next ten minutes Hektor listened without interrupting. He stood up and paced the room. He said scathingly,

'Surely you cannot be serious about the reason for Al-din's criminal activity here, in particular the reason he is so interested in me- I had nothing to do with his uncle's comatose state- I, in fact, was long gone! No, if I didn't know how professional you people are, I would believe that this is some kind of bloody joke! Al-din wanting revenge for me leaving Kyrenia and in a way precipitating his uncle's state of health! What utter madness. I thought he was a respected businessman not a psychopath!' Hektor sat down again and picked up the file, flicking through it.

The powerful looking man opposite, code-name Black Stallion, said determinedly, 'Kyrios Xanthis, I realise much of your activity in promoting the no-vote in the referendum has been behind-the scenes, however a lot of people are aware that you have been a major guiding force- ' as Hektor looked ready to interrupt Stallion held up his hand and said, ' Al-din, you see, would like to see you dead not only for the past but for the present- Have you heard of the Nabucco pipeline?'

At Hektor's negative shake of the head, Stallion carried on, 'The Nabucco pipeline is a proposed natural gas pipeline that is planned to transport natural gas from Turkey to Austria, via Bulgaria, Romania and Hungary. Some consider the pipeline as a diversion from the current methods of importing natural gas solely from Russia. Once completed, it would allow transportation of natural gas from producers in the Middle East and Caspian Region such as Iran, Azerbaijan and Turkmenistan and to the countries along its path, terminating in Austria. The Nabucco pipeline is the EU's answer to reducing dependency on Russia for its gas supplies – and Al-din wants in on it!

He is already on the board of several trading organisations in Northern Cyprus- as you know

Northern Cyprus is unable to trade directly with Europe – nevertheless trade continues through corporations set up by Al-din in Turkey but its costly and involves a lot of greasing of official palms. Al-din is into a lot of suspect deals but the gas pipeline is all above-board- the piece de resistance to make him accepted by the Turkish hierarchy! For several months, in fact, since the project's feasibility study was granted last year, Al-din has been muscling in, hoping to get appointed on the board of directors- so far, he has not managed it but we feel sure it's only a matter of time.

Al-din desperately needs Cyprus to accept the Annan plan for reunification. He then sees Turkey and Northern Cyprus' acceptance into the EU as a matter of course- and all those lucrative contracts coming his way and naturally his business empire expanding a hundred-fold!

As we both know, the problems which face Turkey when the Greek Cypriots enter the EU and the Turkish military occupation question is not settled include the fact that the European Court of Human Rights will hear multiple, ongoing lawsuits against Turkey. The lawsuits will address Turkey's illegal seizure of Greek Cypriot properties in 1974 and will automatically impinge on Turkey's international credit rating, borrowings and inward investment. As well, failure to achieve settlement would automatically disqualify Turkey for entry itself into the EU. Do you see why Al-din and extremist elements within the Turkish Government have you in their sights?

Hektor interrupted, 'I see why he considers me a threat. Nevertheless, he appears to be unhinged as he must know that I am not the only one advocating the 'no' vote- he would have to come after half the government of Cyprus for doing the same thing!'

'I agree' said Stallion 'but coupled with your shared past and the misguided blame he's placed at your door, we believe he is very keen to see you and your family hurt. Sir, we advise the utmost caution.'

Hektor was steely eyed, he paused for an instant and said sternly, 'What prompted your department to disclose this information. You obviously have known about it for some time. Why tell me now?'

For an instant there was a slight look of discomfort on the face of the man sitting opposite. He looked Hektor straight in the eye and said, 'I am extremely sorry to encroach on your private life but recent events leave me no choice. Matters have come to a head! I believe you know a Miss Catherine Burkert?'

Seeing the dangerous look on Hektor's face, the man opposite set his jaw and continued, 'Yes we have known about her for some time - So does Al-din! His men have been on her trail, we are not sure if they initiated the tracking in London but we are certain of it here. Kyrios Hektor, the reason we believe it is imperative that you are fully informed now, is our conviction that you are about to be blackmailed! We believe Al-din thinks he has found uh-uh your Achilles heel-a way to get to you, in the form of Miss Catherine Burkert. With the referendum only a couple of days away-'

Hektor sat deep in thought for a moment, he then said abruptly, 'I believe I have the authority to inform you that Al-din might not just be concerned about the referendum. Turkey will be putting operatives in place if they become aware of us lobbying for the US Bill on the Armenian Genocide,' he explained briefly.

Black Stallion, his lips thin with displeasure said, 'I will inform the department to set up a contingency plan of protection, for all the key members of the government who are in the know. They might be targeted. I wish I had been informed earlier'

He was interrupted by the sound of the telephone on the desk. Hektor frowned and answered the phone, 'I thought I asked not to be disturbed.'

He listened for a moment and said, 'Put him through' Hektor listened to the voice on the other end for a few minutes.

He said tautly, 'I have a man with me at the moment who will know what to do. I will call you back in the next couple of minutes'

Hektor put down the phone and said, ' Mavros epibitor,(Black Stallion) the person you were just talking about, Miss Burkert, seems to be in some kind of danger. One of my men was following her...'.

Hektor related the details.

Black Stallion stood up, 'I will get onto it straight away. Kyrios Hektor, until we know precisely what this is all about, we suggest you do not meet Miss Burkert or contact her in any way. We believe she will be used to get to you and by stopping communication with her, at least until after the referendum, you will be isolating yourself from any harm'

Hektor said, 'If I can be assured that you and your department will be monitoring her and ensuring her well-being, then I will be happy to temporarily cease communication with her. I will make one stipulation- that you keep me informed!'

The other man nodded and left the room. Hektor called Stelios and spoke briefly.

Chapter 19

Abdullah and Mehmet, the occupants of the old green Merc were right behind Cathy as she went past the prisons. Abdullah braked sharply as Cathy started to slow down. Mehmet said, 'Look it's the British High Commission on the right- that's where she's heading-'

At Abdullah's curse he added, 'Should I phone Istanbul?'

Abdullah responded harshly, 'Immediately!'

As Mehmet dialled the number, Abdullah shot ahead of Cathy's car which was being parked. She was getting out. Abdullah parked the car out of her sight and listened to Mehmet as he explained to Igor what was going on.'

Mehmet handed the phone to Abdullah, 'He wants to speak to you.'

Abdullah was unprepared for the icy rage spilling out of Igor's mouth, 'We are not getting through to Burkert. There is no print-out- we don't know what the fuck she is thinking of. Mallard appears to have found a way to circumvent her thoughts. This is not good. The channels are down. I repeat the channels are down. We have to recover them.

Okay, you Abdullah and you Mehmet, keep following her- you will have to use the old technique- switch on the audio equipment, so you can hear the conversation within the High Commission. Is Fatima and the van following you?'

Abdullah turned a little pale, He said, 'Actually I told Fatima to rest this morning. She had an all-night session with Burkert and needed a break.' The next instant Abdullah held the phone away from his ear in order not to hear the harsh, vituperative language from Igor.

Abdullah interrupted and said, 'Don't worry, she can be here shortly'. A minute later he switched the phone off and wiped the sweat from his brow. He dialled Fatima's number.

The man sitting within the embassy in a small room with banks of technical equipment around him put his headphones down and left the room. His job included monitoring the close environs of the High Commission. He needed to see his superior straightaway. The British High Commission's sacrosanct domain was about to be infiltrated by listening devices.

Cathy, meanwhile had tumbled out of the car, and headed for the walled courtyard of the British High

Commission. There were a couple of people in front of her heading towards the gates. They were imposing looking wrought –iron gates with a turnstile which opened electronically. The people ahead of her were let through and then it was Cathy's turn, once the security guard had a good long look at Cathy.

The next instant Cathy was blurting out, 'I need to see someone immediately. My life is in danger!' Tears slipped down her cheeks.

The guard looked at Cathy imperturbably. He said, 'Do you have any identification?'

Cathy rummaged in her handbag breathing rapidly. She handed her passport over. She whispered, 'Please, I must see someone- I'm being followed.'
The guard was taking down her details. He said, 'Well. Miss, they certainly can't get in here without me knowing about it. Hang on a minute and I will see if I can get hold of someone to see you. Although you really should have made an appointment.' He picked up the telephone.

Cathy was suddenly grateful for his prosaic manner. He didn't seem unduly concerned by her words of being in danger. The matter-of-fact English tones calmed her. She waited with hands gripping her handbag. Her head was feeling very strange. It felt like a vacuum in her mind- no speech by third parties- just a huge yawning gap for a few minutes, then thoughts tumbling through her head- she was picking up all sorts of information from around her, naturally like she used to do before. Yes, exactly like she used to before—but my god, there was a difference- her intuitive senses had increased a thousandfold, her mind felt as if volts of electricity were shooting through it. She was picking up stuff about Hektor, about someone called Al-din, a conversation- 'Oh Matt, what are you doing? Are you including in me some new telepathic loop?' she thought dazedly.

The guard put down the telephone, he said, 'Go through, Miss. Did you see the sign about leaving your mobile phone in the car?'

Cathy said, 'Yes. I did'. He gave her a number on a piece of paper. Cathy went in through the door into what was obviously a waiting room- there were a couple of people there- Cathy looked at the grilles noting that it was the consular and visa section- there was a woman behind one of the grilles and Cathy approached her.

Cathy said, 'Can I see somebody urgently? I really need to talk to someone in authority.'

The woman said, 'Miss Burkert, yes, Rawlings at the gate informed us of your request. Someone will be seeing you very shortly. Please take a seat.' She smiled reassuringly.

Cathy sat down, noting inconsequentially that the seats were made of leather. She noticed the door on the left. Presumably she would be interviewed through that door. She felt like screaming because her head felt so awful. The blankness in her mind after the incessant speech with the tapes were running made her feel very ill indeed. 'Is that why her brain was trying to fill the gap by tuning in to other people's thoughts?' 'Where was the healer? Matt, please help me' she said over and over in her mind.

The woman behind the metal grille of the visa section was looking at her oddly. She was picking up the phone. Cathy stared at her through the grille trying to focus on something, her skin felt on fire – what was happening? Cathy could see the metal grille bending and twisting – the woman behind was exclaiming and talking rapidly into the telephone, Cathy could not tear her eyes away from the grille, the metal bars were twisting out of shape – was this in her mind or was it actually happening? Was she, Cathy, doing this? The woman, the embassy employee, had put down the phone and had come through the side door to the front. She was telling the people in the waiting room to stand and move to the back of the room. She was saying, 'We might be experiencing a minor earthquake, that is why the bars have twisted. In a moment you will leave the room and assemble outside until it's safe to return'

A man and a woman entered the room from the door on the left and after inspecting the grille, spoke to the woman from the visa section, she shook her head several times to their questions, the next minute the couple walked up to Cathy and indicated for her to follow them. They were outside in the open air and were walking to another part of the building. Cathy was led to a room and left to enter it alone. When she entered she saw why. There were seats facing another barred grille. Cathy took a seat and saw the couple enter and take their seats on the other side of the barred partition. They introduced themselves. Cathy attempted to smile nervously. The man whose name Cathy did not catch did not return her smile but the woman, Mary, smiled reassuringly at Cathy.

Mary said, 'Tell us a bit about yourself and what are you doing in Cyprus? Do you live here permanently?

Cathy shook her head and explained the reasons for her being in Nicosia. Cathy did not wait for a response. She began without preamble. She said, 'I'm sorry but I need to inform you that my life was threatened and I am being followed' Tears slipped down her cheeks, 'The absolute worst bit is that I am being brainwashed'

'Do you know who is doing this?' said the man For the next two hours they listened to Cathy. Cathy told them everything apart from one detail-

When she talked about the machine and made an attempt to describe it, the embassy man questioned her closely, whilst Mary the woman, took notes. Cathy was relieved that they did not laugh at her. At least they are taking me seriously, she thought.
Cathy mentioned the names she had heard in her mind. She told them about the Turkish contingent and the information she had picked up just today. Hektor talking to someone called Black Stallion, someone in the police, all about a man called Al-din. Cathy

repeated the conversation she had heard, almost word for word.

The embassy man interrupted, 'Are you saying that you heard all of this in your mind?'

'Yes' said Cathy, 'I'm a telepathist.'

'I see' said the man expressionlessly.

'If you don't believe me, please confirm this is true with the psychic healer Matthew Mallard. He will back me up '

'Is Mr. Mallard here in Cyprus? Do you have his phone number?'

'Well, he was here but I'm not certain anymore and no, strange isn't it, I have never thought to ask him for his number.'

'Do you hear him in your mind like the others, Miss Burkert?'

'Yes, I told you, we are both telepathists but I also see him physically. Try him in England. I'm sure he's in the phone book. After all, he is world-famous as a healer.'

'And Mr. Xanthis - you say he is a business acquaintance?'

Cathy nodded. She decided to omit a tiny detail- that she and Hektor Xanthis were lovers. Instead she described him as a business acquaintance who had used her services as an interpreter on a couple of occasions. Cathy her voice anxious and stressed said, 'I cannot convey the absolute urgency I feel, it is imperative to warn Mr. Xanthis of danger- you must act quickly!' She carried on describing how she had been continually threatened if she , herself, did not! Cathy concluded her account, sounding young, disorientated and bewildered. 'I cannot understand how such a machine could be used on people's minds. I have never heard of the existence of such a device, have you?'

The embassy man opposite looked at her imperturbably. He said, 'Can I have the telephone number of the Professor heading your team here? I will need to speak to him to verify a few things'

Mary said kindly, 'Miss Burkert, Cathy, please don't worry, just let me write down the names of the people who you have come across through this machine. So far the prominent ones seem to be Mr. Xanthis, yes naturally we know Mr. Xanthis. We don't know a Mr. Al-din or Mr Mallard – a healer did you say? The others you mentioned- you say they are the people who work for Mr. Al-din? Right, we will be investigating all of this. You can feel safe now that it is in our hands.'

Cathy stood up. The embassy man was making notes. Cathy handed him a piece of paper on which she had scribbled Malcolm's number. Mary smiled and said, 'We will be in touch. Take care how you go now.' Cathy walked out and felt a great burden lifting from her shoulders.

Cathy got into the car and sat staring at the shattered windscreen. She felt utterly drained. Her phone was ringing. Cathy answered it. It was Stelios, sounding agitated and concerned. Cathy spoke calmly and said she was alright. 'Everything is going to be absolutely fine from now on, Stelios. Please tell Hektor I am alright and I will be in touch soon. Goodbye'

Cathy started the car and turned it around heading back to the hotel. The Englishman in the car following behind spoke into his receiver, 'Yes he could see an old green Mercedes but there was nobody in the car. Looks like it's been abandoned- windows down and doors wide open- tell the Cyp's to check it out. Don't make too big a deal of it though. I happen to know the sight of the High Commission's guards making an appearance out front chased them away!!

I'll take over now and follow her. I believe she's on her way back to the hotel and Mary, set up a meeting with Black Stallion. We need to know why one of our British citizens has been targeted.'

Chapter 20

Professor Malcolm Grant switched off his mobile and placed it bemusedly on the desk in front of him. He said to the man sitting across from him, 'Andreas, my friend, that was the British High Commission, we may have a problem.'

Dr. Andreas Michaelides, the head of the department of Antiquities in Cyprus, said 'Another one? What is it this time? I know, he added chuckling, the British must have the stolen papyri in their possession, eh Malcolm- a latter-day Lord Elgin has made off with our precious fragments and they are now artefacts in the British Museum like the Parthenon marbles!'

Malcolm allowed himself a sheepish grin. 'No, no, as you know there is still no news about the papyri- hence the need for us to set up a meeting to decide what's to be done- No, this is to do with one of my team - Miss Burkert- Cathy! The chap from the High Commission- a Nigel Brainthwaite - implied it was quite serious.' Michaelides waited for a moment for Malcolm to enlarge on the story but he did not.

Malcolm was frowning and all Andreas heard him say was, 'Curiouser and curiouser' before he stood up and walked to the door, saying, 'Andreas I have to talk to this chap at the High Commission this afternoon. We shall have to reschedule the meeting we set up. Please inform Tessa. Will call you later'

Meanwhile, Cathy was back at the hotel. She contacted the car-hire company and explained about the accident- no doubt they would let her know if she had to pay any excess- they agreed to collect the car later that morning. Cathy stood by the lifts waiting to ascend to her room. She was picking up all sorts of information, quite disjointed- she knew Malcolm needed to get in touch with her for one. Cathy turned back to Reception and asked if he was in the hotel. Whilst they were checking, Cathy checked her mobile for messages, whoops there were about five- two were from Malcolm, there was one from George, Hektor's minder, one from her mother and another from her flatmate. Just then reception informed her that there was no answer from Malcolm's room. Cathy left a message that if he should return to the hotel, he should get in touch with her. Cathy decided to go upstairs to the room and make some calls.

Cathy felt almost light-headed, telling the British Embassy everything had relieved the immense pressure she had been under. She could still hear conversations in her mind, fragmented, at times inaudible, something to do with police activity, both in English voices and in Greek Cypriot – she recognised the dialect- plans to round up Turkish individuals, were they Dr. Hayat, Abdullah, Mehmet and Fatima? she wondered ?

Thank God she couldn't hear them anymore. Their voices had been stilled since sometime this morning. No more double channels in her mind. No more of being used as a conduit.

What had happened? Matt, she thought, it was Matt Mallard who got rid of them. Darling Matt!

Suddenly, Cathy felt waves of exhaustion wash over her. Her lack of sleep over the last few nights was beginning to take effect. Cathy reached her room and lay fully clothed on the bed –she would make her telephone calls in a couple of minutes. Her eyes closed and she was asleep.

Cathy slept fitfully for the next two hours. She seemed to be semi-conscious with an awareness of activity being conducted at some remote level- in the greater distance of her mind, her psychic energy had not ceased, images swamped her vision, – a siren was sounding, it was a Cypriot police car following a pick-up van, the van was not stopping it was moving very quickly towards a border post- could she see the name of the area – was there a road sign, yes there it was- Famagusta. The guard at the gate was waving the car down but it was heading straight for the barrier. Good God was it going to crash through it? The police car with its sirens blaring was hot on the tail of the pick-up, the guard at the gate was gesticulating wildly! Cathy could make out the face of the big burly man behind the wheel of the pick-up, she recognised the bearded face, she had seen him before – he was slowing down, he was stopping. Cathy could now see another occupant in the front, a young man- his face looked familiar too- a memory of a hospital. The policeman, together with the guard, were indicating for the occupants to exit the car. They got out and started to run to the side of the road.

      Cathy turned restlessly in the bed. Something else was happening.... She could see a face in her semi-conscious state, was it Matt Mallard- his face looked blurred, indistinct – he was on the telephone, what was he saying? Could her mind tune in to his? After all they were connected telepathically, hadn't he told her so over and over again?

Suddenly Cathy drifted to wakefulness. She felt an overwhelming sense of sadness- an utter, unadulterated depth of loss. She felt the healer's presence – the desolation was connected to him, had something happened to him? Was he in danger or suffering in some way? Cathy got out of bed – she wrapped her arms around her body and walked out to the balcony of the room. There was a chair and a table out there. Cathy sat down and stared unseeingly into the distance.

The hotel telephone rang in the room. Cathy quickly moved inside. 'Miss Burkert?' said an unknown male voice – the caller had a Greek accent- Cathy answered in the affirmative. The voice introduced himself, 'I am Yiannis Theodoulou- I work for the police department of Nicosia.'

Cathy's mind immediately went into overdrive. The British Embassy had obviously contacted the police. Had they apprehended the Turkish villains who had invaded her mind? Did they need her to identify them? But she had only heard their voices, and those could have been manipulated by technology, how about the machine or machines? She had only been able to tell them about the electromagnetic fields hoping they would be able to pinpoint exact locations based on her whereabouts.

'Miss Burkert, are you there? said Yiannis Theodoulou

'Yes, I am listening' answered Cathy breathlessly.

'We need you to come to the Nicosia police station. You are from the British University, yes, and you are working with the Department of Antiquities, yes?

Cathy answered in the affirmative. Her mobile phone was ringing. She said to the policeman, 'I can be at the police station in an hour. Is that O.K?'

Cathy on hearing him assent put down the phone and quickly picked up her mobile. Hektor's voice sounded, deep with that special timbre that pulled at her heartstrings. 'Hello' he said – the next instant the phone went dead and there was a knock on the door.

Cathy said, 'Hello, Hello into the phone but to no avail. 'There must have been a fault on the line' she thought, 'he will ring back in a minute.' The knock sounded again on the door. Cathy hastened to answer it.

A chambermaid stood at the door holding a piece of paper. Cathy took it and went to her handbag to give the girl a tip. Cathy couldn't help wondering if this was the same maid who was the last person to enter Tessa Bank's room before the papyri went missing. Cathy, trying not to stare suspiciously at the girl, handed her the gratuity and shut the door. She opened the note- it was from Reception. Whilst she had been on the phone, her mother had called from England. She needed to get in touch with Cathy. Would Cathy call her back?

Cathy looked at her watch. She was due at the police station in one hour and she needed to leave the hotel now to get there on time, taking into account the traffic at this hour – office kickout time.. Cathy decided that she would make the call to her mother in the taxi, on the way to the police station. Cathy took the stairs to Reception- she knew she would be unable to get any signal in the lift and she was hoping that Hektor would call back. God it seemed to be ages since she had last spoken to him. Had the British Embassy informed him of the evil Al-din? Had they told him that it had been her, Cathy, who had supplied the information?

Perhaps he had rung to let her know that he had got the information and was taking precautions- oh she hoped so! 'Please ring back, Hektor' she thought anxiously. She resolved that if he hadn't rung by this evening, she would do the usual and call his bodyguard's number and ask for Hektor to return the call.

Would he though? Cathy knew that Hektor would be very very busy at the moment- what with the referendum only a couple of days away- the latter was obviously on most Cypriots' minds because Cathy heard references to it constantly in her mind. She was picking up the information in Greek, naturally, as she always used to do – no machines, thank heaven!

Cathy was in the taxi on the way to the police station- traffic was busy- she considered with quiet amazement, Hektor's words when they had last met of being groomed to be the next President of the Republic of Cyprus- would he be beyond the reach of ordinary mortals like herself? Suddenly the bubble of euphoria that had engulfed her after she had laid her burden in the lap of British officialdom, burst. She felt utterly deflated and quite wretched- intuitively she knew there was something dreadfully wrong happening somewhere. Her mother, Cathy remembered -she must call her!

Cathy dialled the number. Across town the MI6 operative attached to the High Commission was being briefed by Nigel Brainthwaite, the High Commission's senior official who had interviewed Cathy.

The MI6 operative had a vague resemblance to Woody Allen, thought Brainthwaite, not at all James Bondish- Brainthwaite concluded his analysis on the Burkert interview with: 'I am sure you are aware that British Government policy is totally in favour and have supported for many a year the Turkish application to join the EU fold. We need the referendum by the Greek South to be in the affirmative. Therefore the apprehension of certain Turkish individuals by the Cyps on charges of spying are not convenient at this time- we cannot afford a scandal which could result in a hue and cry by the public , swaying opinion even further from the 'yes vote'. I have informed the Cyps that there will be no charges made by us against those Turkish individuals for monitoring her majesty's subject- uhuh Miss Burkert-whether the Cyps choose to incarcerate the Turkish contingent in some hellhole and throw away the key is none of our business.'

Looking at the faint smirk on Brainthwaite's face, the MI6 operative thought how much he disliked this arrogant little shit- he hated the expression CYPS too- Brainthwaite was so far up his own arse! However, his face impassive he said, 'I can inform you now that we have been aware of Miss Burkert for the last six months. We were tipped off by the Cypriots (He emphasised the word) who were watching the comings and goings of certain Turkish radicals. We had no idea about thought-control devices, though. We have known that such technology does exist but the Yanks went to ground on the stuff some years ago, with the result no info surfaced - Any news on the machines that Miss Burkert mentioned? Have the Cypriots discovered where they are?

'I thought that was your department, old boy! Recovery of apparatus for the glory of Britannia and all that' Seeing a certain indescribable look on the face of the man opposite and sensing imminent danger, Nigel Brainthwaite smiled sickly and said hastily, 'We didn't tell the Cyps everything Burkert told us. We left the mind-controlling machines out of the equation- over to you now. Although, I wouldn't be surprised if the Yanks are playing us off on this one. The Cyps probably know the entire bloody tale and are keeping mum, watching us get our knickers in a twist. Anyway, here are the transcripts of the conversation with Burkert. I have also been asked to tell you that the CIA man here in Cyprus has requested a meet.'

'What is the procedure regarding Cathy Burkert?'

'Ah, well, I have a meeting set up with the Professor in charge – a Malcolm Grant- within the next half-hour. We will be informing him that it is imperative that his young colleague gets a great deal of rest and recuperation. We will suggest that she is sent back to the UK asap- my assistant is organising flight tickets as we speak, where she will receive treatment at a specialised centre- one designated by us.'

Brainthwaite smiled and added, 'You know old chap, we know the drill in such a case. Cathy Burkert will never know the truth.   This region is too sensitive at the mo. We don't want a public hue and cry, a few knuckles will be rapped and that will be the end of that' he shrugged and walked to the door, 'C'est la vie'

Cathy sat across from the policeman Yiannis Theodoulou. Her mind was still full of her conversation with her mother- apparently her mother was thinking of moving back to Italy to be closer to her sister- why didn't Cathy consider making the move as well? After all, said her mother, 'It's not as though you have a boyfriend or anything to keep you in England, dear' As to the question of a job, her mother had an answer there too- 'why didn't Cathy teach English to local Italians, there were plenty of businessmen who wanted to better their English- 'quite lucrative, I'm sure' It was the final bit of information that Cathy was dwelling on, the fact that her brother had been suspended from his job with the airline- he'd been told this morning- the reason he had been given was that he was believed to be drunk on duty! Cathy shuddered with guilt, she had been so intent on getting to the embassy, she had forgotten the threats against her brother- she must call him and tell him to fight the suspension- she forgave him for his indiscretion to Dr. Hayat, he had no choice.

Young Yiannis Theodoulou looked at the beautiful girl with the big green eyes- sad eyes- he gazed at her and wondered in true Lothario fashion, typical of the males in the region, if she would like to go out on a date with him? He decided he would lead up to the suggestion in due course but first to the business at hand. He cleared his throat and said, 'Miss Burkert, we were hoping to speak to Professor Grant or Miss Tessa Banks but they were not answering their telephones. So we asked you here to tell you that we have carried out our interviews with the hotel staff and they all deny knowledge of the missing papers- CCTV in the hotel shows there was one maid who entered Miss Banks room that evening but after questioning her, we believe that she did not take anything- although she might be lying- so we are keeping an eye on her.

Cathy interrupted him, 'I'm sorry, I thought you had called me here for another reason- you see I was at the British Embassy today and I have informed them of certain Turkish individuals who are involved in a plot- I cannot say anymore but I believe the embassy would have informed your superiors-' Cathy looked at his puzzled face and thought he was obviously too low in the pecking order to be informed of political skullduggery!

She hastily said, 'Never mind all that, you were telling me about the papyri, if it's not the maid, who is it? And why wasn't this information relayed over the phone?'

Cathy didn't hear his answer for at this point, Cathy was debating whether she should mention the healer and his pilfering of the missing papers to the policeman. She decided against it.

She merely said, 'It's very important we get them back, you know, for without them we will have no proof that Homer wrote the *Cypria*, not to mention the *Odyssey* and the *Iliad!*'

The young man across from her watched her eyes change as she was speaking- they now had a sparkle. 'Ah a woman who loves her work' He quite forgot what she said about Turkish plots and said, 'I am very sorry but we have not been able to find the papers but we are now checking all the rubbish collected from the hotel- perhaps that will turn up something. That is what we wanted to tell your team- that we are still looking. Do not worry, we will find these very important papers'

He was just about to put on his most charming smile and ask her out when her mobile phone rang- she spoke only the words- 'Straight away. Goodbye' before hurriedly getting out of her chair and saying 'Well if there's nothing else? I have to go you see. It's urgent'.

Cathy was out the room and heading for the entrance. Malcolm had sounded extremely anxious. He had insisted she drop whatever she was doing and return to the hotel immediately. He would be waiting for her in Reception.

Chapter 21

Professor Malcolm Grant saw the lovely slim figure of his assistant enter through the swing doors of the hotel. She looked okay, he thought. He approached her and took her by the arm and led her to a couple of seats in the corner. He did not want anybody else to hear what he had to say to Cathy.

Cathy looked at his grave blue eyes. She started to tell him about the latest bit of information she had just received at the police station regarding the missing papyri- that the chambermaid was being watched... Cathy did not get a chance to utter a word because Malcolm held up a hand and said softly and with deadly seriousness-'My dear Cathy, I have just come from the British High Commission. I believe you were there early this morning?'

Cathy looked taken aback, 'Have they told you why I was there?'

At his slow nod, she said, 'Oh Malcolm I so wanted to tell you what was happening- but I could not utter a word- they were threatening me you see- they had machines- remote devices operating on two different channels- the Turks and the North Cypriots- I am telepathic you see- I can hear and sense stuff from other people's minds- I could always you know since I was little- but this was different , it was terrible, so awful I could not think above this stuff they kept feeding through my brain- at first they were just torturing me and brainwashing me but it changed and I felt very ill...'

Cathy trailed off because Malcolm was looking at her with great pity, 'That's exactly what you are Cathy, very ill-Your mind is sick, you need help urgently.'

'Oh no Malcolm in fact after going to the British Embassy- I mean British High Commission I feel much better- practically back to my old self- even' Cathy leaned over and whispered conspiratorially, 'back to picking up stuff naturally, no blasted machines- lots of talk about the referendum.' Cathy held up a finger and tapped the side of her perfect nose.

Malcolm said, 'Cathy, there was no machine or machines. My dear, The British High Commission did tell me everything- They explained that you were extremely delusional. The threats, the plots and sub-plots never existed- it was all in your imagination.

There are no Turks, no Northern Cypriots, watching and listening to you nor are they monitoring your mind through some remote device. Cathy, each and every bit of your story has no substance. Technology, such as the machine you described, the Embassy explained does not exist! I am so sorry Cathy'

Cathy bristled, 'Nothing to feel sorry about. My mind is perfectly alright- I am not ill. Why, all you have to do is ask Matt Mallard- he will corroborate everything- he will explain that he built the machine, the Turks stole it from him you know- Matt built it specially for us- he will tell you that we are the only two in the world who are able to be conduits- that is why he used me to get to this paedophile and help him- just ask him- Cathy 's voice rose slightly, 'Why haven't the Embassy spoken to him?'

Malcolm took hold of Cathy's hand, he said, 'Hush, my dear try and be calm, I know this is very difficult to accept but the Embassy did get in touch with this Mr. Mallard. He was at his clinic, yes that bit was true, he is as you say a healer but- Cathy- he says he has no knowledge of you. He says he has never heard of you, never met you, never spoken to you, telepathically or otherwise- What's more, laughed at the idea of a machine that could enable thought transmission.' Malcolm held on to Cathy's hand as she turned ghostly white and started to sob.

'How could he deny me? He is my alter-ego you know'

'Have you ever met him Cathy? To speak to like we are now-seated across from each other speaking?'

'No, no, sobbed Cathy but we could communicate telepathically and I could always see his physical presence, like an aura, sepia- tinted outlines- oh its hopeless trying to explain'

'All of it wasn't true- he suggested you might have known of him because he's published a few books on the art of healing. Is that where you saw his photograph - on the cover of a book? You must know that would have provided the physical aura you could see.

But Cathy was holding her hands over her ears, she was crying and was starting to get hysterical- 'What about the woman Fatima who was brainwashing me? She can confirm she hear Matt speaking in my flat. She told me so. She did, she did!' Cathy sobbed in an intensity of emotion.

Malcolm shook his head and said quite firmly, 'Cathy, there is no such person, you imagined all of it- the machine, being watched and listened to by Turkish people, entire conversations, you are very ill indeed...'

Cathy interrupted him, 'How about Hektor Xanthis? You know the politician – he's also a big name in shipping? Malcolm please tell me that the Embassy warned Hektor of the plot against him? Did the Embassy believe that information, at least?

'My dear, take it easy, all they said was that because of your mental condition, you would be prone to create scenarios involving people you met – I believe you knew Mr. Xanthis briefly- no Cathy you have got to understand that you cannot make up stories involving the top echelon in Cyprus and implicating Northern Cypriots and Turks, especially as matters stand at the moment with the referendum looming in the next couple of days'

Cathy got to her feet, she wrapped her arms around her body and muttered softly, in between sobs, ' That's precisely the reason they want to get to him because of the referendum- he and his family are in danger- they spoke of doing harm to his wife, his son - I must warn him. I must'

Malcolm said placatingly, 'Cathy listen to me if it were true, you have no proof! Nothing apart from stuff you heard in your mind. Don't you see how crazy all of it sounds?'

Cathy stopped sobbing and tried to pull herself together- although little gasps escaped her.

'Malcolm I gave them the name of the man who is behind all of this- a Mr. Nasr Al-din. He spoke of 'fucking Xanthis up a bit! There's the proof- surely the British Embassy could investigate HIM because I know he's real. I just know it!'

Malcolm chewed his lip and shook his head at her, 'I know the name actually – no not from the Embassy- oh, Cathy, my dear he's been in the papers recently, something to do with gas and oil being piped via Turkey- don't you see the name must have lodged in your memory. Come now, my dear- no more of this..'

Malcolm took her arm and said quietly, My dear, I have been trying to prepare you- a doctor is waiting here for you. She will give you an injection which will calm you and help your disturbed state. I've spoken to the doctor and she thinks extreme stress has brought about your condition- she mentioned you were probably experiencing some kind of psychosis- She will accompany you to your room where Tessa is waiting. Tessa has packed your clothes- there is a flight back to England tonight- you will be met at Heathrow and taken to a facility- just for the night and the next day you will have an appointment with a psychiatrist- in no time you will be on the road to recovery! Don't worry about a thing.'

Cathy removed Malcolm's hand forcibly from her arm, she took a deep breath, wiped her eyes and said with a degree of calm, 'I'm alright now- it was just the shock you know of you telling me that it was all in my imagination' Cathy hoped that Malcolm would start to be convinced that she'd accepted his words but inwardly, in her mind and in every fibre of her being, she knew she had not imagined anything! She could not be mad, could she?

No, no, no, it had been all so real- the Turkish voices-Matthew Mallard- the machines- God, if the British Embassy did not believe her, then Hektor was a sitting duck. Already they had carried out their threat against her brother. What would they do to Hektor? I must get word to him. She said aloud, 'I must go to the loo – tidy up' Cathy walked to the toilets. Out of the corner of her eye she could see Malcolm signalling to a plump Cypriot woman- the doctor, thought Cathy. The doctor was heading to speak to Malcolm. Cathy realised she did not have much time as she was sure the doctor would follow her. She shut herself in a cubicle and quickly dialled her flatmates number.

Alison answered with a 'Thank Goodness- I've been calling you as I haven't heard from you for yonks- are you alright, lovey?'

Words tumbled out of Cathy's mouth – she heard someone enter the toilets- Cathy pulled the flush, hoping it would drown out her whispered words. Cathy quickly ended, 'I can't say anymore- you know what to do, Ally'

Cathy stepped outside the cubicle and began to wash her hands. The woman Malcolm had beckoned to came close beside her and said, 'My dear, I am a doctor. We will now go to your room where I require you to lay down for a minute or two. I will give you an injection- it will help you a lot- and you will tell me the stories that have been going through your mind- all the conspiracies- and then I will accompany you to the airport and stay with you until you board your flight.

You will be perfectly fine- nothing at all to worry about.'

Cathy said nothing at all. She walked to the lifts with the doctor beside her and they duly entered her room where Tessa was waiting - Cathy lay on the bed still not speaking whilst the doctor busied herself getting the injection ready- Cathy looked at Tessa, felt the prick on her arm and closed her eyes. The doctor tried to talk to her but Cathy would not speak. The silence lasted all the way to the airport until Cathy boarded the flight. She was aware of a man sitting next to her on the plane but Cathy's head was so woozy, she just closed her eyes. She was so very, very tired.

When the aircraft landed, a man – an immigration official, he explained and a woman in nurse's uniform, shepherded the somnolent Cathy through the terminal, past the usual checks- in the back of her mind Cathy thought the British Embassy in Cyprus had certainly prepared for a smooth handover- Cathy next felt another prick in her arm, administered by the nurse who smiled and uttered reassuring platitudes, felt herself being driven in a vehicle to a building with green walls inside and a room with a bed, which looked comfy. 'I must sleep' thought Cathy and closed her eyes.

Alison, Cathy's flatmate, had been unable to sleep. She lay in bed and looked at the clock for the umpteenth time. It was 4 a.m. – God she was so worried about Cathy - Gentle Cathy- what on earth had she got herself into? When Cathy had phoned her yesterday evening she had duly dialled Xanthis' number just as Cathy had instructed- but there was no answer. Alison had put the phone down and pondered the message Cathy had instructed her to give Xanthis. Beware of Nasr Al-din- he means to hurt you or your family, take great care. Cathy had then rung off abruptly.

'What the devil was going on? And why couldn't Cathy herself tell Xanthis? Then just as she had picked up the phone to redial Xanthis' number - Alison's phone had then begun to ring, she had hurriedly picked it up, thinking it might be Cathy again with an explanation, but the voice at the other end was clipped with a posh accent- 'Nigel Brainthwaite from the British High Commission in Cyprus-nothing to worry about- your friend Cathy Burkert paid us a visit at the High Commission here, she is fine apart from being very confused. She is in now the care of a doctor who believes she is experiencing a form of psychosis-a mental illness where delusions occur- she is on her way to the airport and will be in England in a few hours. We have arranged for somewhere for her to stay for the rest of the night.

One of my assistants will give you a call as to when and where she can be collected from. Oh Miss, Alison if I may, if you have heard from her in the past hour, please discount anything she might have told you- the lady needs a great deal of support and help in the coming weeks and as her friend, you I'm sure would want to offer that. Under no circumstances should you encourage her fantasies as it is essential that reality sinks in- do you understand?'

Alison had blurted out, 'She called me earlier- she didn't seem right. What should I do regarding Xanthis- she insisted I was to warn him about a man-' Alison looked at her piece of paper on which she had jotted the name down-'a man called Nasr –Al-din- he means to harm Xanthis'

Braithwaite said calmly, 'Miss Alison as I said earlier, Miss Burkert is very delusional.

These are the names of people she has been reading about in the press- I realise she had an acquaintance with Xanthis but she is really imagining all this- she is currently being treated and you will see that she will be starting to feel more like herself in a few hours and will be able to dismiss all these fancies. In fact I guarantee that by the time you collect her from the recovery clinic tomorrow, she will not be able to remember much of what she has been saying.'

Alison felt reassured, 'Poor old ducks', she thought. In the next instant Alison had wished Braithwaite goodbye with the assurance that she would be free to pick Cathy up from the recovery clinic.

But the feeling of calm had not lasted long and Alison had lain awake until this hour feeling quite bothered. She did not know much about mental illness, never having come across it before. 'Poor Cathy, she must be going through hell with her mind feeling as though it's being invaded. Unimaginable torture as the mind is such a sacred personal entity!'

Brainthwaite had said Cathy was delusional and that she had plucked names out of a newspaper but thought Alison- 'Xanthis is Cathy's lover, - the old granddad as Alison would tease Cathy, not a mere acquaintance as Brainthwaite had said.

Cathy had opened her heart to Alison telling her about all the doubts and guilt she felt sleeping with a married man. Cathy had even told Alison about the shivery sensations when she just thought about Xanthis and how apparently Xanthis had owned up to feeling the same – Alison remembered thinking that it was all pretty weird talk but she had accepted that such phenomena could possibly exist.

But now- my god- how far back did the delusions go- had Cathy been mentally ill for a long time? Worse still, did Cathy actually know this man Xanthis? Had she made up the entire story of being his lover? Had she Alison listened to over twelve months of make-believe?

Chapter 22

'This surely is a road going nowhere,' thought Cathy, as she trudged the gentle sloping terrain of a hill in Tuscany. Gnarled olive branches caught her eye as she turned the corner and at last, thank goodness, there was Aunt Francesca's lovely old stone house. The taxi had dropped her off at the end of a very long, narrow road – too narrow for cars -and she felt weary after the long walk. Her suitcase weighed like a ton, her feet were sore but she felt a renewed joy deep within her, something that had been very lacking in her life lately.

Momentarily dismissing the last 6 months, she saw smiling faces at the window and the next minute she was being hugged with exclamations of 'So good to see you, cara' 'You have gone so thin' They crowded around her, the cousins and her aunt and ushered her into the warm living room with its terracotta tiles and bright yellow walls. 'You should have told us when you were arriving, said Paolo Moretti, the eldest cousin. 'We would have picked you up. Papa has had to go into town with your Mama but they will be back in time for lunch. I am sure you are longing to see your Mama as she is longing to see you– she has talked of nothing else recently'

'Picked up a flight at the last minute' said Cathy as she sat on the russet sofa, sinking gratefully into it's depths, 'so couldn't give you advance notice and yes I can't wait to see Mum.'

Two hours later, with the entire Moretti family present including her mother Lucia, and having exhausted all the news relating to each member of the boisterous clan, and answering with a degree of shame their careful enquiries as to her state of health, Cathy was told to go for a shower and get freshened up before lunch.

Standing under the shower, Cathy felt a memory, a faint recall of doing exactly the same thing in another warm climate- Cyprus – it seemed such a long time ago, yet it had been only six months- the medication dulls the sharpness and grief of those early days, reflected Cathy. Cathy quickly stepped out of the shower as she felt the old familiar pain of loss- benumbed by the tablets she was taking - as were all of her other emotions, but nevertheless constantly there. She had learnt to fight the ever-present depression.

Depression and shame that being diagnosed as mentally ill had made her feel.

The stigma of mental illness was almost unbearable especially when people close to her, like her relatives, asked concerned questions- Cathy felt that they looked on her as an alien in their midst, an object of pity, someone who looked and sounded perfectly normal but had heard 'voices' and was delusional!- not quite sane.

People generally take comfort from being the same as each other, not like me! I've been proved to be different. I wish I was like them, thought Cathy dejectedly – I don't want to be psychic or psychotic, telepathic or telebloodykinetic.

The psychiatrist who Cathy had seen for a few sessions had told Cathy not to attach self-blame for being ill but to consider it as any other physical ailment which had to be treated with medication. But Cathy did not believe it was quite as easy as that. For if she wanted a job with the Police or MI6 or the Government, was she employable? Cathy wondered. 'Would she be trusted to be of stable mind, in a position of responsibility?'

'If Hektor knew about me, would he think less of me?' was Cathy's next thought. Cathy still felt heartbroken at the loss of Hektor in her life.

As she finished towelling herself dry she thought with a degree of derision, ' One man, a single member of the male species to cause such heartache- will I ever get over him?'

Cathy, no matter how much she would have liked to believe that her telepathic abilities were lost through the anit-psychotic medication -was wrong, her ESP was alive and well- for at that precise moment, Hektor Xanthis was actually thinking of the young woman who had tugged at his heartstrings. He missed her in his life but there was no going back, he thought. He was still twisted with grief at the tragedy that had befallen his family that he had been unable to bring himself to answer any of the calls she had put through. He could not think of anything and anybody at that hopeless hour. He had achieved everything only to lose the most important part of his life. The referendum had been successful, in so far as what he personally wanted to achieve. The Cypriot South had voted 'no' thanks largely to his, Xanthis' immense efforts whilst the

Turkish North predictably voted 'yes'. Cyprus still remained a divided island.

Xanthis recalled the last couple of days leading up to the referendum as being drawn into a maelstrom of uncontrollable forces. First, Black Stallion the head of the internal security had phoned through that Catherine Burkert had been bundled post-haste on a flight to London by the British High Commission. Very few details had been divulged as to the reasons why-- but Black Stallion had agreed with Nigel Brainthwaite that she was best out of harm's way.

Black Stallion had also reported that the Turkish Cypriot villains had been rounded up and Xanthis recalled there was a strange mention of some items of sophisticated machinery now in Cyprus' security vaults. The Americans, Xanthis heard it whispered, probably CIA, were helping to take the whole lot to pieces to decipher exact functions.

The CIA had also informed Cyprus of Al-din's involvement and Cyprus had decided to convey through certain key figures in the Turkish Government its displeasure at Turkish interference. Deals were struck. Al-din because of his lucrative contribution to the Turkish and Northern Cyprus economies via his business interests, was to go scot-free but his movements would be curtailed and closely monitored for the rest of his life.

Everything seemed to be swimming along.

On April 24th, 2004 the referendum was held and the Greek Cypriots, by an overwhelming majority voted 'no' to the Annan plan for re-unification.

Xanthis had felt a great deal of personal satisfaction at the outcome. That evening at a celebratory dinner, full of laughter and congratulation, Xanthis' minder handed him the phone. Listening to the caller at the other Xanthis felt the blood drain from his face- he was looking into a future so grim, so full of pain, he could not utter a response. Silently he handed the phone back and went in search of his wife. He sat her down in a quiet room and broke the dreadful news to her. Their son was dead. He had been killed in a car crash- a hit and run. He held her for more than an hour and soothed the dreadful cries that were torn from her body. Next he summoned his relatives to be with her. Hektor knew that he had to be on his way shortly to Greece to bring the body back. First, Hektor had to make some calls.

Black Stallion sounded far away. He listened to Xanthis' strained voice and said with deference, 'I am exceedingly sorry for your loss. I am not in the country at the moment but I will head towards Greece within the next day or two to determine the exact sequence of events. It's pointless surmising at this stage. Yes I do realise there were threats made against your family but we cannot say at this time, if your son's death was a result of these threats. Please Kyrie Hektor, be patient and I personally pledge my entire team to get to the bottom of this.'

A month later, Black Stallion, even with whole-hearted co-operation from his dedicated men was no nearer finding out if the crash had been an accident or a deliberate assassination. With great reluctance he headed back to Cyprus. A verdict of accidental death was ruled and Hektor could now begin to mourn his son.

Black Stallion never told Hektor of a subsequent conversation he had with a Cypriot doctor hired by the British Embassy to look after Cathy Burkert. The lady had repeated to him Cathy Burkert's words in a toilet in the Hilton hotel. Cathy had been unaware that the Doctor could hear every word- but the doctor was clear in her recollection- Cathy Burkert had been speaking to someone, to get them to call Xanthis to warn him of imminent danger to his family. How had Catherine Burkert known? The British embassy had maintained that Cathy Burkert was diagnosed as mentally ill, hence the haste to get her back home. 'Was there more to the story?' wondered Stallion. It had been strange that at the same time of Cathy Burkert's hasty departure from Cyprus, the CIA man had informed him of a plot involving Turkish Cypriots, Al-din and machines. The CIA had not told his department what the machines were used for. The information on that had gone straight to the top- The President's ear only.

Stallion's suspicious mind tried to work out all the angles. The only information he had known was that Cathy Burkert was being followed by the Turkish contingent and he had realised and warned Xanthis that he might be the ultimate target. Why machines? Without knowing the function of the machines, he kept coming up against a brick wall. And he knew suddenly that he would never know. It had something to do with Cathy Burkert. Black Stallion wondered if Xanthis still saw the girl. He would not have been surprised if Xanthis took up with Catherine Burkert again- he had seen the man's face when he had talked about her. He had looked like a man in love. Stallion shrugged and put the Burkert episode out of his mind.

Cathy sitting at the lunch table in her aunt's Tuscan farmhouse and eating her favourite clam pasta was having a moment of quiet with all the cousin's chatter around her. Her mother looked at her with concern from time to time. Cathy had been through hell in the last six months with mental illness- had Cathy been ill for years? There had been no signs of it before, not in childhood or in her youth...... but thankfully now she was on the road to recovery. She had been unable to work in the last few months but on this visit to Italy, perhaps she could be persuaded to settle here and look for local employment, thought Lucia.

Her mother resolved to find out about Cathy's last job in Cyprus. Lucia knew that something had gone dreadfully wrong there which had Cathy getting so very ill with a psychosis and delusions.

Lucia said gently, 'Cathy my dear, whatever happened to Professor Grant? Have you heard from him? He called me repeatedly for weeks whilst you were ill. Did you get in touch with him?'

'Strange that you should ask, Mum. I have not spoken to Malcolm recently but he sent me a long letter via email recently which I have yet to read. I printed it out though and have brought it with me and plan to get into it after lunch.'

'Yes, have a rest, my girl, after lunch. It will do you good'

With luncheon over, Cathy curled up on the window seat and took Malcolm's long missive out. He had been so sweet, calling to find out how she was getting on. Unfortunately, they had not been able to keep her post open indefinitely at the University but suggested she reapply in the new term. There was bound to be an opening somewhere for a girl with her talents.

He wrote, 'I know you will be eager to know the conclusion of the Leander and Morpheus fragments and the story of Philoctetes, so I took the trouble of relating in detail the story as it stands. Cathy, as I mentioned to you on the phone- the missing papyri never did turn up, therefore total authenticity could not be reached. However, with the copies we were able to piece together the patterns and rhythms necessary to establish the work as being definitively Homer's.

Here Malcolm went into great detail about Homer's phrases of repetition and so forth. Cathy quickly skipped over them until she reached the Philoctetes section. What had happened to the maiden Halcyone who had cured Philo of his snake-bite? According to Malcolm, when Odysseus came to inveigle Philo to rejoin the Achaean effort to fight the Trojans, Philo would not be parted from Halcyone and moreover he could not be persuaded to leave the island of Lemnos. In desperation, Odysseus swore an oath to the gods that Halcyone would not be left behind. She would accompany them on their voyage to the battlefields of Troy.

On that promise, Philo consented finally to join the Achaean side.

The sea-voyage to Troy was fraught, as storms and gales were constant and the ship was buffeted night and day with torrential rain and high winds. The crew grew very tired and unhappy. There were mutterings amongst them that the bad weather was the fault of the maiden Halcyone. Women were bad luck on board ship. They boded ill and would cause the ship to capsize sooner or later. Odysseus and Diomedes listened to their cries of discontent and wisely said nothing.

One morning Philo woke up to find the sea becalmed. There was no movement and no Halcyone. He raised the alarm but she was nowhere to be found. They searched everywhere and the crew joined in with a show of frenetic energy but they would not look Philo in the eye. They refused to partake in the songs of woe he sung at her disappearance nor did they praise openly the tranquil night sky for bringing an end to the storms. They did so in secret fully justified in their act of throwing the beautiful maiden overboard. They comforted Philo and vowed that henceforth they would attach a figurehead to their boats- a wooden effigy carved in Halcyone's image. And that my dear, is how the first figurehead was probably attached to the mast of a ship, wrote Malcolm, all in the name of the beautiful maiden Halcyone. Philo went on to take part in the Trojan war, killed Achilles...well, you know the rest Cathy.

As to the Morpheus and Leander accounts –you were quite right in saying that Morpheus' writings did in fact prove that he was present at the recital although Tessa's Leander's was a second-hand report.

My dear Cathy, I cannot begin to state the loss of such papyri to History and to posterity. For without it nothing can be proved. We know it exists so does the Laboratory in Greece where the fragments were carbon-dated but someone has stolen them. Someone is sitting gloating over them even as I write this to you. May he rot in hell'

Cathy put the letter aside and thought immediately of the healer. She knew he had taken the papyri but having heard him confess to the deed only in her mind, there was no way she could inform on him. She had tried to tell people the truth of what had happened in Cyprus but nobody believed her. Everybody in officialdom had thought it had all been in her mind. They had thought she was mad! And she had had to believe that what they said might be true. Perhaps she had been delusional- perhaps she was, as they said, psychotic!

Cathy clutched the cushions of the seat and figured out why she had started to doubt herself- why she had started to think she might be psychotic, even though deep within her she knew she had not imagined what had happened in Cyprus, why then had the doubts crept in and rooted themselves in her mind?-

'Because... because the healer had denied her very existence- had denied speaking to her in any way. My god, he had said he didn't know her at all. The shock of his rejection was so unbearable, even now, six months later. Cathy felt utterly forlorn for not only had her relationship with Hektor broken up, (he had not answered any of her calls and she missed him desperately)- but Matt, her confidante and healer had rejected her.

Cathy's mother was calling out to her. Cathy went downstairs. The family were going for a walk. Would she like to join them? Cathy agreed with a yen for some fresh air. It would get rid of the cobwebs.

For the next few days Cathy debated staying on in Italy. But in the end, regretfully she knew she had to go back to London. The answers to all her questions lay somewhere in England. For Cathy had decided she wasn't going to be labelled as a psychotic- she was going to prove that she was as sane as the next person. She was going to prove that the events that had taken place in Cyprus were as she had stated, not just in her mind but hard, cold reality.

First she had to find the healer- he was the access-point to the machine, the machine that had enabled her to be a conduit, the healer knew everything, she was sure if she came face to face with him, he would recognise and acknowledge her. She must find him.

Chapter 23

THREE YEARS LATER

Matthew Mallard sat at the breakfast table with the newspaper in front of him. He was up earlier than usual as he knew he had a busy day ahead of him. The list of patients at the surgery was particularly long as he had to include an extra patient who was in urgent need of treatment- a mental illness case. The case seemed interesting- a young girl. Italian, by the sound of the surname. He hadn't had to attempt treatment on a mentally ill patient before so this presented somewhat of a challenge- he was looking forward to trying to heal the girl.

In the meantime he sipped his cup of coffee and looked at the headlines. The Russian President Vladimir Putin was more than likely to take over as head of GAZPROM the Russian gas and oil giant, when his term of office was finished. Gazprom had its sights set on creating new pipelines, via Greece through to Europe, so the paper was reporting. What would Europe say about that, wondered Mallard – Europe, having gone to considerable expense in investing in the

Nabucco pipeline via Turkey. Surely they would never let Russia in through mainland Greece as that would ensure that Russia would have almost a total stranglehold on the energy markets.

Mind you, thought Matt genome research might make nonsense of gas and oil in the future, as he remembered an article he had read recently. Research using the genome- the genetic code of organisms- The Americans were way ahead on that one- transmuting one species into another by transferring just the genetic code- it represents only the first step towards man-made organisms, thought Matt.

Matt recalled reading that the goal is ultimately to design new organisms that fulfil specific functions such as manufacturing new fuels to replace oil and gas or capturing carbon dioxide, without evolving so that these capabilities are locked in over time. The Americans hoped to create fuels from such an engineered organism within a decade or less. Although, according to some, the Americans especially the MIT lot, had a time-scale for development much closer than that. Probably the clever dicks have it up and running already, keeping the rest of the world guessing, thought the healer.

Mallard's extra-sensory perception was extremely acute. Mallard had homed in a sense of national pride. For when the CIA man in Cyprus, John Harper, read the recent updates on the intel from MIT, he felt huge pride in his country. 'Good ole US of A' he said aloud.

'Genome Research had paid off- man, whilst the rest of the world were mired in the oil and gas political play-offs, especially the Ruskies- we are sitting on (to use the MIT man's words) red, hot and smokin' technology! The same words had drifted through Mallard's mind, establishing the telepathic loop, as he had read the article on genome research.

In a very small article on an inside page, a name sprang out - Why, it was the arch-villain Nasr Al-din? Thought he had been finished off after the Cyprus fiasco? Mallard had heard through a contact in the British High Commission in Cyprus, three years ago, that Al-din would never be allowed to leave Turkey because of his attempts to interfere in Cyprus politics. Obviously things have changed because here's a picture of him courting GAZPROM. Wonder if MI5 have picked up on that story. Better ring Brainthwaite in Cyprus just to make sure.

Nigel Brainthwaite answered the phone on his desk. It was the healer, Mallard. Brainthwaite was friendly. He had reason to be friendly, for three years ago when Cathy Burkert had walked into the British High Commission and claimed that a Matt Mallard was involved in highly suspect dealings to do with minds and machines, Brainthwaite had rung Mallard to question the authenticity of Burkert's story. Mallard had admitted to some of it and since the Turkish contingent had been rounded up and had confessed their part in the rest of Burkert's story, Brainthwaite and his superiors had decided not to haul Mallard over the coals for using illegal means to invade a person's mind. In exchange for something - Mallard struck a bargain- He would give up all the machines and related info and something else-He had something in his possession of great value to the British government. Ancient papyri virtually authenticating Homer's great writings was now safely in British hands, housed in a remote underground vault along with other precious artefacts.

Mallard had been a tremendously useful chap. Brainthwaite had never told Mallard that his superiors had thought it prudent that Burkert should believe she was mentally ill and undergo treatment accordingly.

Instead Mallard had been informed that she was now working for Hektor Xanthis and was closely involved with him on a personal basis. Mallard had seemed rather upset but never had reason to doubt the story.

Brainthwaite thought about the information the CIA man Harper had given Her Majesty's government including Xanthis' involvement in the Bill being put forward to the US Congress just this summer. The Cyps needed to drive a wedge between the US and Turkey, what with all the clamour for Turkey to be included in the EU. They had set things in motion three years ago -What better way than to use the US propaganda machinery - and they had so nearly succeeded this year, 2007. However, proponents of the Bill condemning the Armenian genocide were almost guaranteed certain victory next year, despite Turkey's attempts to scupper the congressional recognition. Xanthis, to all appearances, could not put a foot wrong politically. Although since losing his son in a tragic accident (Brainthwaite recalled how Burkert's prediction had come true, although it had never been proved that Xanthis' son's death was anything more than an accident) Xanthis had stepped down from his presidential ambitions.

'Wielding influence behind the scenes, no doubt' thought Brainthwaite. Especially now with talk of a new referendum to be held in Cyprus within the next twelve months. Britain hoped to use its influence to promote mutual recognition between the North and the South of Cyprus for all were in agreement that recognition was the ignition key- moreover recognition at grass-roots level - of individual flags of North and South Cyprus rather than host countries like Greece and Turkey, recognition of a united Cypriot front at international games and competitions- bloody hell, the list was endless. British interests would be served, thought Brainthwaite if Cyprus were to unite. First, we've got to get the Cyps to work out the Turkish-occupied land issues.

Nigel Brainthwaite's mind worked furiously as he rubbed his hands whilst speaking to Mallard on the speakerphone. He had fed Mallard, from time to time, certain titbits of information and now it seemed to be paying off for here he was again being a loyal subject of her majesty- yes Brainthwaite said, they had picked up on the story re: Al-din and he was being monitored closely. Everything was in hand and thank you very much.

Brainthwaite depressed the button on the speakerphone, bringing the conversation with Mallard to a close and thought of Al-din with satisfaction. Another one on Her Majesty's payroll. It had taken some doing lifting the embargo on Al-din which the Turks had insisted on after Al-din had taken matters into his own hands without his government approval three years ago- the Cyps too had to be heavily persuaded not to go after the man for interfering in Cyprus politics. 'All for the greater good' Brainthwaite had said to Black Stallion. 'We now have a man on the inside, straight to the Russians. We believe he was so hogtied by the Turkish authorities that he was willing to do anything to break free. Even giving up his vendetta against Hektor Xanthis. Yes we wrung a sort of hands-off approach out of Al-din. He knows on which side his bread is buttered!'

Mallard of course knew nothing of this. Matt Mallard put the phone down and walked the short distance to the surgery. By mid-morning he was reminded by his secretary of the new patient. She had just arrived and was waiting. Matt asked for her to be shown in.

Cathy di Laurentis Burkert walked in to the room and stared straight into the healer's face.

Her mind was in tune with his. Now she knew everything. Everything, that the world would believe was a creation of her diseased mind. Her green eyes were sparkling emeralds in the perfect face. She felt the electricity sizzle and her whole being felt supercharged. The feeling of Liquid Gold. The hair on her arms was standing on end. She held out her hand and he took it. She said, 'Hello, I've wanted to meet you for a very long time'

THE END

Bibliography

This book is a work of fiction. However, the names of the scientists and quotes on their subject matter are real.
Dr. Kevin Warwick – online source
Dr. Robert Becker – online source
J. F. Scapitz – online source

IN ACKNOWLEDGEMENT
Professor Chris Railton - University of Bristol –
Professor in Computational Electromagnetism
I also wish to acknowledge Homer's genius and the story of the *Cypria*. The story conveyed in the book as written by Homer is largely accurate, but I have taken modest liberties and embellished the conclusion.